OPEN ROADS
BOOK FOUR OF THE EMPTY BODIES SERIES

Zach Bohannon

OPEN ROADS
Zach Bohannon
www.zachbohannon.com

Copyright © 2015 by Zach Bohannon. All rights reserved. This is a work of fiction. Any resemblance to actual persons living or dead, businesses, events or locales is purely coincidental. Reproduction of this publication in whole or in part without express written consent is strictly prohibited.

Edited and Proofread by:
Jennifer Collins

Cover design by Johnny Digges
www.diggescreative.com

CHAPTER ONE

Somewhere in North Carolina

Will stared down at the wounds on his arm, tracing the lower of the two with his opposite hand over and over again. For as long as he lived, these scars would stand as a constant reminder of just how fucked up the world had become. They'd also memorialize David Ellis; a man who'd done so much to paralyze Will's soul, and had now left his permanent mark on Will's flesh.

Eventually, the others would likely ask Will what it had felt like to die, and he wouldn't have an answer. He'd only seen black. There were no lights, no angels strumming harps, no endless sea of white clouds. Nothing but darkness. And he'd had no sense of just how much time he'd spent *in* the black. One moment, he was lying on the road. Then he was gone. And when he'd woken up again, he had no recollection of what had happened in between. Perhaps, he thought, he'd been in some sort of purgatory.

After the time spent at the farm burying their friends and then regrouping, Will had remained mostly to himself, fighting an internal battle to try and come to some kind of realization and acceptance of what had happened to him. Others in the group had noticed the change in his demeanor, and silently offered him his space. This included Holly, even though each time Will looked at her he could tell that she was on the verge of emotionally breaking, obviously wanting so desperately to help him.

The group had managed to find a vehicle once they'd made it near the interstate. They'd chosen a minivan which had been left at a gas station. The key to it sat right on the passenger seat. The gas pumps at the station itself had been empty, but for whatever reason, the van had remained untouched by looters, and the fuel gauge on the dash had sprung to three-quarters full once the engine had roared to life. Jessica had suggested that it was perhaps by faith that they'd found the perfect vehicle. Bullshit, Will thought. Because faith had been the question with no answer since he'd woken up.

Including the front cab, the van had three rows of seats. Jessica rode up front with Gabriel, who was driving. Holly sat on the middle bench, keeping the two children entertained. Dylan was almost back to his normal self, or at least the version of 'normal' that he'd created since The Fall, and Mary Beth seemed to be coming out of her shell a little bit. Will sat in the back, alone. Every now and then, Holly would turn around and flash him a smile, which he'd vaguely return. Part of him felt guilty for shying away from her at such a strenuous time, but he appreciated her patience while he sorted things out in his mind.

With night creeping upon them, the group found themselves becoming desperate. The three-quarters of a tank just wasn't enough. They'd made multiple stops to try and find more fuel, but had only been able to scavenge a few gallons. If they couldn't find more gasoline soon, they'd be forced to walk again. This wasn't an option.

"It'll be sundown soon," Jessica said. "We need to start finding somewhere safe to stop for the night."

"I just wanna drive a little longer," Gabriel said.

"I know you want to get home, but if we run out of gas, especially when it's dark, we won't be able to get to Washington any quicker. We've got to find somewhere to stop. You know that's the right—"

"You don't think I know what's 'right'?"

"Guys," Holly said from the middle aisle. "Stop it. There's no point in arguing." She drew in a deep breath. "Jessica is right, Gabriel. If we get stuck in the night with no gas, we may not be around to—"

Holly paused, looking over at the children. They were listening intently now, no longer distracted with whatever mindless games she had been able to amuse them with. She was relieved to have held her tongue, not wanting to worry them with thoughts of the group being stranded in the dark of night.

Gabriel sighed. "Be on the lookout for a good place to stop."

"I know a good place," Jessica said. "I'm fairly familiar with this area. It'll be better than where we stopped last night and it's only a few exits away."

The previous night, the group had stopped to rest at the last gas station where they had searched for fuel. The plan had been for Gabriel, Holly, and Jessica to take shifts on watch, but Will had insisted they let him take the first shift, even though everyone in the group had felt he'd just needed to rest. He'd ended up staying awake most of the night, remaining on high alert the entire time. During his watch, Will had seen a small pack of Empties lumbering across the street, but it had been too dark for them to notice the minivan sitting in front of pump #4 on the other side of the road. He'd eventually given in and had allowed Jessica to take a shift, as he'd become tired and realized he would do more harm than good to the group if he fell asleep while on watch. They'd survived the night unscathed.

"Take this exit," Jessica said.

"Where are we going?" Gabriel asked.

Jessica looked over to him and smiled. "You'll see."

Gabriel shook his head. "I hope wherever you're taking us is safe."

***

The sun was quickly making its descent when the van came to a stop. Will shifted to where he could look out the opposite window and leaned down to see the building sitting at the top of the hill.

"That's perfect," Holly said.

"As long as no one is up there," Gabriel said, sounding unsure.

"Only one way to find out," Jessica said.

The sign read: Tar Heel Storage. A rod iron fence surrounded the entire property, and it sat on top of a hill, making it a perfect place for the group to hide from Empties. Even if the creatures could make it up the steep hill, the fence would certainly keep them out.

The front gate was shut, which Will knew could be either good or bad. Good, because nothing would be able to get to them once they were on the other side. Bad, because it was possible that another group of survivors had already claimed the storage facility.

Gabriel cut the wheel and headed up the driveway. He stopped the van in front of the fence and rolled down the window, examining the security keypad.

"No power," Gabriel said.

"No surprise there," Holly said.

"Let's see if we can open the fence manually, Gabriel," Jessica said.

Gabriel nodded, and both he and Jessica stepped out of the van.

Holly turned back to Will. "How're you doing?"

Will forced a smile and nodded. "Fine."

He could sense that she was disappointed with his short answer, but the children were both happy now, and the way this conversation would likely turn wouldn't do anything but hinder the mood of the kids. They'd been through enough already.

A few moments later, Gabriel and Jessica arrived back at the van. They each opened one of the sliding panel doors on either side of the van.

"We'll have to jump the fence," Gabriel said. "The power's off and that gate isn't budging. It's not going to open without power."

"Well, at least we should be safe once we get inside," Holly said.

"Grab some bags, guys," Gabriel said to Dylan and twelve-year-old Mary Beth. "Get what you can, and we'll toss it over the fence."

"I can't climb good," Mary Beth said.

"It's okay, sweetie," Holly said. She ran her hand through the girl's hair. "We'll help you get over."

Everyone helped in transporting supplies as they stepped out of the van. The kids grabbed the pillows and blankets they'd taken from the old farmhouse, and Will was sure to get the small gas can from the back. It had about a gallon left, but every ounce of fuel mattered, and they couldn't afford anyone breaking into the van overnight and stealing it.

Two of the bags were small enough to fit between the fence's spaces, and Jessica transferred those to the other side, squeezing them between two of the rods. Gabriel tossed the others over the eight-foot fence, only having to throw one of the bags more than once; it took him three tries to get the duffle full of canned food over the top. He kept the bag containing most of the guns and ammo over his shoulder, planning to just climb the fence with it. For now, he set it down on the ground.

"You go first," Gabriel said to Jessica. "That way, you can help the kids from the other side. I'll give you a boost."

Gabriel kneeled down and cupped both his hands together, creating a base. Jessica stepped into his hand and he boosted her up as she caught hold of the top of the fence. Gabriel held her balance as she swung her leg over and jumped down onto the concrete, inside the fence.

"Alright, bud," Gabriel said, looking at Dylan. "Your turn."

Gabriel helped Dylan boost himself over the fence, followed by Mary Beth and Holly.

Will approached the fence and handed Gabriel the plastic red gas can. He secured the bag on his shoulder, then looked up to the top of the fence. Will grabbed onto the rods, and pulled himself to the top. Once there, he sat with a leg on either side, and handed the bag down to Holly.

"Give me the can," Will said down to Gabriel.

Gabriel handed Will the gas can, which he in turn gave to Holly. Then Will hopped down from his perch at the top of the fence.

Gabriel pulled himself up, and joined the group on the other side.

Reaching into the bag of weapons, Will pulled out two handguns, handing one each to both Jessica and Holly. He threw one of the rifles to Gabriel, and grabbed a shotgun for himself.

"Let's look around," Will said. The sun had hidden behind the horizon, so he kneeled down to one of the other bags and pulled out the three flashlights they'd found in the farmhouse.

Will kept one for himself, then handed one to each of the women.

"Do I get a gun?" Dylan asked.

"You don't need a gun, buddy," Gabriel said. "We'll watch after you."

"But I can watch after myself."

Will half-smiled, a gesture which the group hadn't seen in what seemed like a millennia. "I know you can, buddy." He signaled Dylan to follow him and they stepped away from the group. He leaned down to the boy and whispered, "You need to look after Mary Beth. She's scared, and you having a gun would just scare her more. We are all strangers to her except for you. So, you need to help her stay calm. Can you do that?"

Dylan nodded.

"Good," Will said, rubbing the boy's shoulder.

They re-joined the group, and Will looked to Gabriel and said, "Alright, let's do this."

CHAPTER TWO

Tar Heel Storage was made up of three buildings. Two of them had blue metal doors every few feet, for the entire length of the structures. These were the outdoor units. The third building had a single glass door, and a sign on the outside read: Climate Controlled.

Gabriel slipped the rifle's strap over his shoulder and headed toward the two buildings of outdoor units. He stood in the middle of the lot, rows of doors on either side of him. Pointing the flashlight at the doors to his right, he noticed that all of them were closed. Each unit he focused the flashlight on still had a padlock in tact. The others in the group approached him from behind.

"Isn't it a little bit strange that all these doors are closed?" Holly asked. "Wouldn't you think that some of these people would have, at least, come by here?"

"It's kinda out in the middle of nowhere," Jessica said. "Maybe none of the tenants could make it here."

"Or maybe they just didn't need anything from here," Will added.

"It sounds like no one is here, but let's look around to make sure," Gabriel said. He looked over to Jessica. "Stay back with the kids; Will and I will take the lead. We'll head straight down here, and check behind the back."

Jessica nodded and holstered her gun in the back of her pants.

"Come on, guys. Stay close to me," Jessica said. She put her hands out and each of the children grabbed hold.

Moving a few yards in front of Jessica, Holly, and the children, Gabriel and Will started down the middle of the two buildings. Gabriel shone the flashlight back and forth between the two buildings, as well as in front of them. The moon provided some light, but not enough to give them much assistance. Each unit he shone the light on looked untouched. They seemed destined to each be their own time capsule, not to be opened for years.

They came to the end of the row and reached the fence again. Gabriel looked to Will and whispered, "Take Holly and head around the far side of this unit." He pointed to the building to his right. "I'll go this way with Jessica and the kids, and we'll meet you at the door of the climate controlled building."

Will nodded, and he put his hand on Holly's back to lead her around the side of the building. Will pulled his hand away from Holly and readied the shotgun, pointing it in front of him, as Holly used the flashlight to illuminate their path.

"Where are they going?" Dylan asked.

"Shh," Jessica whispered, her finger to her lips. "They'll be right back."

Gabriel put his hand out toward Jessica, signaling her to hang back with the children. Checking to make sure it was clear, he peeked his head around the corner of the building, flashed the light down the back side of the structure, and saw nothing. He looked back to Jessica and nodded for her to follow.

They moved around the back of the building and the main office came into view. It was connected to the climate controlled storage building, but sat at the back of the property where they now stood. Gabriel narrowed his eyes. He put his hand back again, urging Jessica to hold the children back.

"What's the matter?" Jessica asked.

Gabriel turned back and whispered, "There's a car parked over here. Stay back with the children."

He crept toward the vehicle. It was a large SUV, parked in one of the spots near the office. He pointed the flashlight at it and saw that it still had the dealer tags on the back, and then he shone the light through the back window. Aside from some clothes in the back seat, the truck appeared to be empty.

Gabriel heard footsteps at the end of the row and quickly turned away from the SUV.

"It's just us," Holly said from the front side of the property.

Gabriel relaxed and waved them toward him. Jessica must've heard Holly because she came around the corner with the kids and walked over to the SUV.

"Anything inside?" Jessica asked.

Gabriel shook his head. "Doesn't look like much. We'll give it a better look later."

Will and Holly arrived at the truck, and Holly stroked the side of it.

"Damn, this is nice. Too bad we can't get that gate open and drive this outta here."

"There's still a chance that whoever owns this is here," Gabriel said. "We've gotta stay on our toes and check inside this building. If someone is inside, they could very well already know that we're here."

"I checked the door to the climate controlled units on the way over here," Will said. "It's locked. We could easily break in, but we should check inside the office first. Maybe we can find a key."

"Good idea," Gabriel said. "You and I will check the office. Jessica and Holly, you two keep a look out here and stay with the children."

The group nodded in unison.

Will walked over to Holly and handed her his shotgun. "Take this and give me the handgun."

"You sure?" Holly asked.

Will nodded. "If you guys get into trouble, it'll be better for you to have this. Gabriel has the rifle. We'll be fine."

Holly nodded.

Will looked over to Gabriel. "Let's go."

***

The glass shattered as the butt-end of Gabriel's rifle slammed through the office's front window. He reached around, unlocked the door, and opened it. Will snuck by him and entered the office first, aiming his gun in front of his face.

"After you," Gabriel mumbled, and used the flashlight to illuminate the room.

The office was simple. A desk sat in the middle of the room with all the essentials on top: a computer, phone, notepads, scattered papers, and pens. The wall nearby displayed various packing supplies that the facility sold, such as boxes and tape. There was a coffee machine and microwave sitting on top of a small table on the other side of the desk. Behind the desk, there was a single door. Will went to the desk.

"Come 'ere and give me some light," Will said. "Maybe there's keys in one of these drawers."

Gabriel hurried over to the desk and pointed the flashlight as Will opened up the top drawer and rummaged through it. He searched each drawer, throwing papers and other things all over the ground. When he'd looked through each drawer, he sighed and looked down to the ground.

Gabriel furrowed his brow. "You doin' alright, man?"

"I'm fine."

"You sure?"

Will narrowed his eyes. "Let's just keep looking around." He turned toward the door behind the desk.

Gabriel shook his head and shined the light onto the door as Will pushed down the handle. It clicked, and Will pushed it open, entering the room. Gabriel shined the light inside the space.

To the left was a set of stairs. Gabriel shone the light to the other side of the room and saw just how small it was. A cleaning cart with a mop and bucket sat against the wall, but that was it.

"You hear that?" Will asked.

Gabriel stood still and listened.

"Hear what?"

"Come on," Will said, and he started up the stairs. Gabriel reached out and grabbed onto Will's shoulder.

"Easy," Gabriel said. "If there's someone, or *something*, up there, we need to be quiet so they don't hear us coming."

Will stared at Gabriel for just a moment, then nodded. Gabriel entered the room behind Will, and pointed the flashlight up the stairs.

"Holy shit," Gabriel said.

Blood stained the wall in the shape of human handprints. Gabriel moved the beam up the wall, and the same stains decorated it every few feet. He shone the light down onto the stairs, which also had blood on them. He whipped his head toward the top of the staircase when he heard a snarl.

"Hear it that time?" Will asked.

"Let's just be careful."

Will nodded in agreement, then turned to move up the stairs. The steps were made of metal, making them easy to mount without making much of a noise. Eight stairs up came to a landing, and then five more stairs to the right led to a door. The familiar hiss was prevalent now.

"Sounds like it's just one of 'em," Gabriel whispered.

Will crept up the stairs and gently turned the handle. He looked back to Gabriel and said, "It's locked."

"Let's just turn back and leave it in there. It's trapped in that room."

Will shook his head. "It's probably the live-in tenant. I bet we'll find the keys in here, and maybe some other goods." He moved back down the steps and joined Gabriel. "Stand back and give me some light."

"Will, no," Gabriel hissed.

But Will had already decided on his next move as he charged up the stairs and threw his shoulder into the door. Gabriel darted up the stairs behind him, and shone the light inward as the door fell into the room, and Will with it. It must've gone down easier than Will thought it was going to, because his momentum carried him all the way to the ground.

The beast snarled, but Gabriel couldn't see where it was.

"Here!" Will yelled.

Gabriel pointed the light down and saw the hands coming up from each side of the door.

"Shoot it!"

Gabriel saw Will's pistol had fallen onto the ground near him, and he hurried to pick it up. He positioned himself at the top of the door where he could see the creature's head peeking over the top. Gabriel used one hand to point the light down at the beast's head, and aimed the gun with the other; then he pulled the trigger. Blood shot up as the bullet entered the thing's skull.

Will rolled off the door, onto his back. "Thanks," he said, gasping for air.

"Pretty lucky that he was right on the other side of the door," Gabriel said.

Will reached over and moved the door out of the way, and Gabriel directed the light to the Empty's face.

"*She*," Will said, correcting Gabriel.

Downstairs, the door to the front of the office creaked opened, then slammed shut.

"Are you guys okay?" Jessica called. "Where are you?"

"Up here," Gabriel replied. "Through the door behind the desk."

They heard footsteps come up the stairs, and the two women and children appeared in the doorway.

"Will," Holly said, and she rushed to his side.

"I'm fine. No worries."

Gabriel moved the door the rest of the way off the Empty, and tilted his head. He pointed the flashlight at its waist and he smiled. Kneeling down, he grabbed something off the creature's pants.

"What's that?" Will asked.

Gabriel flashed the light on the object he held up in front of his face, revealing the dangling keys to the rest of the group.

***

The third key that Gabriel tried opened the door into the climate controlled storage space.

"Will and I will go in first," he said. "Stand back and give us plenty of light."

Gabriel pushed through the door, and Will followed close behind. Each of them readied their weapons, prepared to face any threat. Once everyone was inside, Gabriel put his finger to his lips, urging the others to be silent, then signaled for Holly to point her flashlight ahead of them. The air was filled with silence, aside from the five of them breathing. Ahead, the hallway appeared vacant, lined with blue, metal doors on either side which all looked to be closed. Gabriel turned to the right, and the women followed him with the light. He looked down another hall of similar length, its scene exactly the same.

"I think we're clear, but we should look around," Will said.

"Agreed," Gabriel replied.

At the cautious pace they used, it took them ten minutes to check the building before arriving back at the entrance. As predicted, the facility was vacant.

One of the units near the front door was open. They took a brief look at the items at the front of the unit before deciding they'd check in more detail in the morning when they'd have natural light pouring in through the glass front door. Gabriel wished he had a way to open some of the other units up and look to see if he could find a blanket or something he could use as a pillow. But the kids each had their bedding, at least, and the two of them being comfortable was what really mattered.

"I'll keep first watch," Will said.

"I don't think it'll be necessary," Gabriel said, shaking his head. "The door's locked and we know we're the only ones here. Even if someone shows up, they're gonna have to come crashing through that glass door. We'll just sleep up here; that way, we'll hear if someone shows up."

Gabriel looked over to Will, and he could see the pure exhaustion in his friend's face. He walked over to him and put his hand on Will's shoulder.

"Tonight, we all rest."

CHAPTER THREE

I see the blood stains on the road. I notice the iron substance dripping off a nearby bush. It's almost as if I can smell him. He's here.

And then he jumps out of the vegetation, and I'm taken by surprise. I feel the burn in my arm. The reanimated David Ellis falls, but not before he curses me.

My arm pulsating from the two bite wounds, I lie on the ground alone, looking at the sky. Cold. Becoming so cold.

What's that voice? Who is that?

I don't know who or what it is, but it's inside my head. I can't understand what it's saying. Slowly, it's becoming clearer.

It's the voice of my mother.

"Will... Will... Will."

Her voice sounds so tired and defeated.

"Mom?"

"How could you, William? How could you let him do that to me?"

I begin to cry. "I'm so sorry, Mom. I wish I could take it all back. If I could, I would've just killed myself when I woke up in that fucking warehouse."

"William?"

That's my father's voice. I look to the gunmetal sky, but I see nothing. No face. Nothing.

"Dad?"

"You were supposed to protect her," my father says. He's

crying almost as hard as I am. "How could you fail me like that, son?"

"But, Dad, I—"

"Don't 'Dad' me! You fucked up! This is all your fault! You're a worthless piece of trash, son! You always have been!"

I shake my head and I squeeze my eyes shut as hard as I can. Something trickles down my face, and I put my hand to my cheek and pull it away to see blood. Near convulsing, I rub my eyes with my fingers and can feel the blood flowing from my eyes in place of tears.

Then a laugh. It's familiar, but it's not that of my mother, nor my father.

David.

He continues to laugh as I feel something inside me taking over. All the blood in my body seems to be rushing to my head, and it feels as if two hands are squeezing my brain, like one of those foam stress balls.

Oh, God, what's happening to me?

"God?" David says. "God?"

My eyes widen as I see his face in the sky above me. His eyes aflame, and that laugh.

"I'm your God," he says.

He starts with that evil laugh again, as I find myself gasping for air. My back arches.

I scream, and the last thing I see before everything goes black is the large head in the sky opening his mouth, and coming down to swallow me.

Will awoke from his nightmare in the middle of the scream. It carried over into reality, and he let out a dry, raspy yell. He sat up and saw Holly sitting on the floor nearby with the kids. All three of them looked startled, and Holly jumped to her feet and rushed over to him.

"Are you alright?"

Will lay back down, realizing that he'd shot up too fast and that the blood had rushed to his head. He put his hand to his forehead and breathed in and out in rapid succession.

"Will, talk to me," Holly said.

"I'm fine," Will said. "Really. It was just a bad dream."

The front door opened, and Gabriel and Jessica came into the facility.

"Is everything okay?" Gabriel asked. "We heard a scream."

"I'm fine," Will repeated, still rubbing his forehead, his hand now wet from perspiration. "Just a nightmare."

Will heard a sniffle and looked over to see Mary Beth in tears. Before he could say anything, Jessica went to the children and took their hands.

"Come on, let's go outside," she said, and she led Dylan and Mary Beth out the door.

His breathing back to normal, Will sat up. He used the collar of his shirt to wipe the sweat from his face and let out a long sigh.

"How long have you guys been up?" Will asked.

"Couple of hours," Holly said. "You were sleeping like a rock, so we decided to just let you rest."

Will ran his hands through his hair. "Shit. Guess I didn't realize I was that tired."

"Yeah, well, luckily we noticed," Gabriel said.

Holly looked up to Gabriel and asked, "You guys find anything yet?"

Gabriel nodded.

"What's she mean?" Will asked.

"When I woke up this morning, I went to check out that SUV and went back inside that apartment above the office to see if there was anything up there we could use. The SUV didn't have anything in it aside from some makeup and shit, and it's almost out of gas. The needle is on empty. But inside the apartment, I found some canned food, bottled water, and some nuts. We can't have enough of that stuff."

"Great," Holly said.

"I also found these in the office." Gabriel pushed the door open and leaned outside on one foot, bending over to grab something. He came back in grasping a set of bolt cutters. "We've already busted open a few of the units to see if we could find anything."

"And?" Will asked.

Gabriel shook his head. "We grabbed a few blankets that were being used to cover furniture, but that's about all we found that would be useful. Found a bunch of shit probably worth a lot of money, but I don't see that doing us good anytime soon."

"We probably don't need to hang around here too much longer," Will said. "I know it's cozy, but we need to get back on the road."

"Don't have to tell me twice," Gabriel said.

The door opened, and Jessica moved halfway into the doorway with a concerned look.

"You guys need to come have a look at this."

***

"And you haven't seen or heard anybody?" Gabriel asked.

"No," Jessica said. "I looked around for just a second, then I grabbed the kids and ran back over to the storage unit."

Will walked around to where he could see through the rod iron fence. The driver's side panel door of the van was wide open.

"You sure we shut it last night?" Holly asked. "Who was the last one out of the van?"

"I made sure it was closed," Will said.

"You sure? You were pretty out of it," Gabriel said.

"I shut the fucking door!"

"Whoa, easy," Jessica said, nodding in the direction of the children.

"This isn't helping anyone, guys," Holly added.

Will blew out a deep breath. If there was one thing he was tired of, it was the group babying him over the last few days just because of the shit that had happened. He distinctly remembered closing the door to the van all the way, no matter how exhausted he'd been.

"Let's run back to the building and grab our things," Gabriel said. "If someone knows we're here, it's best we get the hell out of here as fast as we can."

***

The group threw everything over the fence and scaled it, just like the night before. Jessica and Holly went first, and then Gabriel and Will each helped one of the children get over the top. Then the two men climbed over and helped load everything into the van. Considering how much stuff was presumably in all of those storage lockers, the group's haul was minimal. They'd come away with more food and water, a few blankets, some candles they'd found in the tenant's apartment above the office, and a pair of bolt cutters.

Will looked down as he opened his hand. In his palm were the keys Gabriel had found in the apartment above the office, clipped to the Empty's belt loop. Will reared back and threw the keys over the fence as far as he could. He figured that if another group of good people stumbled upon this place, they might need them.

He loaded into the back row of the van. He was the last one to get in, so Holly pulled the sliding door shut beside her.

"Someone was definitely in here," Gabriel said from the driver's seat. "The glovebox was opened and the console is wrecked, and I left a jacket on the floor of the backseat that's gone."

"Let's just get out of here," Holly said, a slight tremble in her voice.

Gabriel slipped the key into the ignition and turned it, but the engine just groaned.

"What the?" he said.

He tried again, and the same thing happened. He slammed his hands on the steering wheel in anger.

"Son of a bitch siphoned our gas!" he yelled.

"Does that mean we're stuck here?" Mary Beth asked.

"I've got about a gallon in this can back here," Will said. "We can't stay here. For all we know, whoever stole Gabriel's jacket and the fuel could have left to go get friends. If that's the case, we don't wanna be here when they get back."

"What about the tenant's SUV?" Holly asked.

Will shook his head. "That gate is far too strong. We'd do more damage to the vehicle than it's worth, especially considering it has almost no gas."

Will passed the can up to Gabriel via Holly, and Gabriel stepped outside to feed the tank with the remains of their fuel.

"What happens if we leave and then don't find any gas?" Dylan asked.

Holly looked at the boy, not sure what to say. And when she looked back to Will, all he could do was shake his head.

He knew that *not* finding gas wasn't an option.

CHAPTER FOUR

The sky was overcast, looking as if it might open up at any moment and bring forth a storm. They'd only driven a few miles down the road, but had yet to come across much resistance in the form of either piled cars or stray Empties.

Successive gasps for air sounded from the middle row of seats. Bodies shuffled, and an aura of panic hung in the air.

"Pull over," Jessica said, glancing over to Gabriel from the seat beside him.

"What's wrong?" Gabriel asked.

"Stop the car!" Holly demanded.

Gabriel cut the wheel, and before the mini-van had come to a complete halt, Holly threw open the sliding panel door on the passenger side.

"Come on, sweetie," Holly said.

Gabriel looked back to see Holly and Dylan assisting Mary Beth with getting out of the vehicle. Jessica opened her door and jumped out, slamming it behind her. Will slid over the middle row of seats to join them outside.

Gabriel opened the door and stepped onto the highway. He scanned the area, realizing they appeared to be the only sign of life around on this desolate stretch of North Carolina freeway. They'd be okay to stop here for now.

He walked around the side of the van, where Jessica, Will, and Dylan stood in a semi-circle. Holly sat on the ground, her arm wrapped around Mary Beth.

"She okay?" Gabriel asked.

"She's having some kind of panic attack," Jessica said. "Probably stress. She's starting to calm down, though."

Mary Beth had her head nestled into Holly's chest as Holly rocked back and forth, and continuously said, "Shh, it's okay."

"Let's just give them a few minutes," Will suggested. He put his hand on Dylan's shoulder, and led him to the other side of the van. His face blush with concern, Dylan turned back and kept his eyes on Mary Beth as Will urged him away.

When they'd moved to the driver's side of the van, Gabriel could see for himself just how upset Dylan was.

"She's gonna be okay, buddy," Gabriel said. "She's just scared."

"It's just…" Dylan's voice trailed off as he wiped at his eyes.

"It's just what, buddy? You can talk to us if you need to," Gabriel said.

Dylan took a moment to gather himself, then he looked up to Will and said, "The way she was breathing… it reminded me of seeing you on the ground after the accident."

"And just like me, she's going to be fine. It's like Gabriel said — she's just scared."

A few minutes later, Holly and Mary Beth appeared from behind the van. Though her entire face was red, Mary Beth appeared to be much happier now. A smile grew on Dylan's face, and he went to Mary Beth and hugged her, an embrace she allowed with her own open arms.

Holly walked past the children to join the adults.

"She's better now," Holly said.

Gabriel leaned in and whispered, "Has she said anything about where she came from or how she ended up at that farm?"

Holly shook her head. "Not to me. I'm not sure what Dylan knows."

"I'm ready."

Gabriel looked past Holly and saw Mary Beth standing there. She reached over and opened the closed panel door on the driver's side of the van, and jumped into her seat.

The rest of the group loaded in, and Gabriel cranked the engine as he buckled his seatbelt. He looked to the gas gauge. The needle hovered around the letter E.

And as he pulled back onto the open road, that's when Mary Beth started to talk.

CHAPTER FIVE

The Day of The Fall
Dawson Home - Maryville, TN

"22, 21, 20, 19..."

Fourteen-year-old Susan Dawson continued to count down from sixty as her younger sister, Mary Beth, looked for a place to hide.

The woods behind their house stretched for what seemed to the children like miles. It was their favorite place to play. Since Mary Beth had been old enough, the two girls had spent hours upon hours playing out here. A bit off the grid, it had always been safe out in these woods; this place was truly the childrens' sanctuary.

Curled up with her knees at her chin, Mary Beth hid behind a large log. Her sister sat on the tree stump about thirty yards away. They'd named the stump 'Home Base'; it was where the seeker always counted while the other went to hide.

"2, 1," Susan said. "Here I come."

Mary Beth stilled her breathing. Autumn was quickly approaching, and the leaves that had fallen to the ground made it easier for her to hear her sister approaching. This was a welcome advantage for Mary Beth, who'd never been very good at hide and seek. Susan routinely found her sister in one of the three spots she liked to hide, but the games almost always lasted longer once Autumn came.

Sitting on the broadside of the log, Mary Beth's nose started to itch. Something in the air had triggered her allergies, and she now found herself trying to hold in a sneeze. She rubbed her nose with the heel of her hand, but it only made the sensation worse. Then, just as Susan's footsteps started heading the other way, Mary Beth sneezed.

She heard her sister's footsteps stop, and instead of waiting on Susan to come get her, Mary Beth revealed herself.

"Dangit," Mary Beth said, crossing her arms in a pout.

"Come on," Susan said, laughing. "We gotta head back so we can finish school." The girls' mother home-schooled them.

"Race you home?" Susan suggested.

Mary Beth bowed her head, signaling she wasn't in the mood to play. But it was all a ploy. Looking down at the fallen leaves, Mary Beth smiled, and then bolted away from her sister.

Both girls laughed as they ran, and Mary Beth could hear that her sister was using her slightly longer legs to catch up to her, the leaves crunching under their feet. Mary Beth was determined to win something today, and chugged her legs harder to try and pull away from Susan.

"I'm gonna beat you," Mary Beth said, smiling as she swung her arms and ran.

But something felt strange. It sounded as if only *her* feet were beating the ground.

Mary Beth stopped running and turned around. Susan no longer followed her. Instead, Mary Beth's older sister lay face-down, about twenty yards back.

"Susan!"

Mary Beth rushed to her sister's side and kneeled down beside her. Susan lay with her eyes closed, her head staring off to the side. Her entire body was limp.

"Susan? Are you okay?" Mary Beth shook her sister's

shoulder, but Susan didn't move. "Please, Susan. What's wrong?"

Mary Beth reached down to grab her sister's wrist and check for a pulse, and Susan grabbed onto Mary Beth's arm and gasped for air. Mary Beth yelled, falling back onto her butt.

"Gotcha!" Susan said.

Mary Beth pulled her arm away and stood, scoffing at Susan. "That's not funny!"

"Sure it was," Susan said. She pushed herself up onto her knees and patted the front of her dress down to knock off the loose dirt and grass.

"You're a jerk," Mary Beth said. She patted dirt off her backside, then turned away and continued to make her way toward the house.

"Come on, Mary Beth," Susan said. "Don't be a baby."

Mary Beth ignored her sister, continuing home. Susan hurried to try and catch back up.

Then Mary Beth heard a thud behind her, and turned around to see that her sister was on the ground again. Only this time, she lay on her back.

"Yeah, okay," Mary Beth said, shaking her head. "Now you're really being annoying." She started to turn away again, but something didn't feel right. She kept her eyes locked onto Susan, closely watching her sister's stomach. Mary Beth waited for it to rise and then fall, but nothing happened; it remained completely still.

Mary Beth crept toward her sister, keeping her eyes focused on Susan's body to see if it would move. The woods were dead around her, the leaves beneath her sneakers making the only sound she could hear. She arrived at her sister's body. Susan lay there with her eyes and mouth wide open, and Mary Beth could see now that she definitely wasn't breathing.

"Susan?" Mary Beth kneeled and shook her sister. Susan's head rocked, but her facial expression didn't change.

Tears rolled down Mary Beth's face, and she shook her sister again. "Susan, this isn't funny! Wake up!"

Mary Beth put her hand on Susan's face, and realized that her sister's skin felt cold. Susan could fake a creepy face, but she couldn't make her own skin feel chilled.

Standing up, Mary Beth stepped back, not letting her eyes leave her sister. The tears flowed more intensely now, and the emotion came to a boil when Mary Beth finally screamed.

She turned and sprinted home.

***

The Dawson house was a quaint, all-brick home, sitting on five acres of land. It had been built on top of a hill, the front yard sloping upward toward the entrance, and the back a steep downslide into the vast woods that covered the land behind the house. Charles and Maria Dawson had bought the 1951 ranch-style house just a year after they had been wed, and they'd hoped it would not only be their first home, but their last.

Mary Beth's voice had been wearing thin, with her screaming all the way home as she raced in between the trees. When her house came into view, she ran faster, gaining momentum to dart up the hill. She used a combination run and crawl to mount the yard, still using her hollow voice to call out to her mother.

She climbed up onto the large wooden deck and blew through the door, not caring that it had swung all the way around on its hinges to slam against the shared wall. She scanned the living room, looking for any sign of her mother.

"Mom! Mom, where are you?"

She ran through the living room and headed down the

hallway toward her parents' bedroom. She heard the sound of water running through the pipes come to a stop, and when she reached the bedroom, her mother came walking out of the bathroom, wrapped in a towel.

"What is it, honey?" her mother asked, concern in her voice.

"It's Susan, something's wrong with her."

Her mother's eyes widened. "Where is she?"

"She's out in the woods! Hurry! You have to help her!"

Her mother moved faster than Mary Beth had ever seen, not caring that the towel dropped, revealing her nude back side to her youngest daughter. Within moments, she had on a shirt and jeans, and had laced up a pair of tennis shoes.

Without hesitation, she took Mary Beth by the hand and raced for the back door.

***

When they arrived at the place where she'd last seen Susan lying face-down, Mary Beth was stunned to find that her sister had vanished.

"She was right here," Mary Beth said.

"Are you sure?" her mother asked. "It's pretty wide open out here. There's a lot of places she could be."

Mary Beth nodded and pointed to the stump sitting in the open with no trees around it. "There's Home Base. We always walk straight out this way when we head back home."

Mary Beth took a few steps forward, then noticed something on the ground. She bent over and picked up the pink, polka dot headband that her sister had been wearing.

"Maybe she went back home," Mary Beth said.

"But you said that you guys always go back the same way that we came," her mother said. "We would've passed her." She sighed and put her hand to her forehead, clearly stressed, and said, "Let's split up and scan the area."

Mary Beth nodded and walked toward Home Base as her mother veered off somewhere behind her, looking for any sign of her sister.

"Susan?" Mary Beth called out repeatedly. "Where are you?"

No response.

A cold, dark feeling crept up inside Mary Beth. Something just wasn't right.

"Susan?"

Leaves rustled nearby and Mary Beth halted where she stood. She looked toward where she thought the noise had come from, and remained still so that she could listen. The leaves rustled again, this time joined by a strange, inhuman sound; it was not so different than the sound of an angry dog.

"Susan?"

A figure appeared from behind a tree, and Mary Beth's eyes widened.

She wore the same dress, the same shoes, and her hair was styled the same. But her eyes, her skin — both were so pale.

Susan lumbered toward her sister, a strange wheeze escaping from her mouth.

This time, Mary Beth spoke in a whisper as she recited her sister's name, once more.

There was no response. The lifeless figure only continued to trudge toward Mary Beth, not seeming to even be aware of where she was or who was speaking to her.

Mary Beth screamed.

***

Two Days Later...

"We simply can't stay here anymore," Mary Beth's father

said. "We've been lucky that we're in such an isolated area, but John told me that it's absolutely chaotic out there." John was their neighbor from next door.

"But, Charles, we have no idea what we're getting into out there," Mary Beth's mother said.

"Yeah, but if we stay here, it's only a matter of time before we run out of food. And then what? What if there's none to be found? Hell, it might already be too late."

Maria Dawson sighed with stress. "Where would we go?"

"John heard from a friend of his that they were allowing refugees onto campus in Knoxville," Charles said, speaking of the University of Tennessee. "He said the football stadium is closed off and they've got a bunch of survivors housed there."

"And what about Susan?" Maria asked. "We can't just leave her here."

"Honey, we can't—"

"No, Charles," Maria said. "I'm not leaving her."

"It's too dangerous, Maria. We have to. You saw her. She tried to bite Mary Beth. And what if whatever is wrong with her is contagious? Do you want to live out the rest of our days without *either* of our children?"

Mary Beth listened in from the hallway as her mother started crying. For two days now, they had been unable to get medical assistance for her sister. Their aforementioned neighbor, John, had been a doctor before retiring some years ago. Shortly after Susan had become ill, John had arrived back home from errands. He'd urged Maria not to leave, and explained that whatever had happened to Susan seemed to have been widespread, and that everyone on the road was in a panic. Instead, he would do his best to tend to her. He hadn't been able to help her, and she'd soon transformed into some kind of monster.

With John unable to diagnose and treat the problem, Charles had tried taking his daughter to the hospital. Somehow, they'd managed to get her inside the trunk of the car, as she'd proven too dangerous to ride in the cab. Two miles away from the nearest hospital, he'd hit a road block, where authorities had been turning people away. The police, trying to control the panic of everyone trying to seek help, told Charlie there was no more room in the hospitals, and that they'd have to turn around and go home.

For a short time, they'd tried to keep Susan comfortable in her bedroom. But after she'd escaped one of the times her father had opened the door to check on her, and then tried to bite Mary Beth, they'd had no choice but to move Susan outside, to the shed in the backyard.

"Maria," her father said. "I'm sorry, I didn't mean to—"

"You're right," her mother said. "We can't put our family at risk like that. We have to try and go without her."

There was a long awkward silence, and Mary Beth looked around the corner into the living room to see her parents embracing. Her mother's shoulders rocked up and down as she cried into her father's chest. Mary Beth's father caught his daughter's gaze and pulled away from his wife to acknowledge Mary Beth.

"Mary Beth, how long were you listening?" he asked.

"We can't leave Susan," Mary Beth said, ignoring her father's question. "We just can't."

Charles went to his daughter, moving his hand to her shoulder, but she stepped back. He sighed and said, "It's too dangerous to take her with us. We'll come back for her. I promise."

"Let me stay here with her," Mary Beth said.

Her mother stepped in.

"Look, sweetie. You heard me. I don't want to leave Susan here either. But, your father is right. It's the only option we have. John is going to watch her, and make sure that she is okay until we can get back here with help for her. She's sick, baby. Too sick to travel. Letting your sister out of that shed would only put us all in danger."

Feeling as if she was being ganged up on, Mary Beth sat down against a nearby wall, bringing her knees up to her chin. She hid her face from both of her parents and started to cry. Part of the reason she was so upset was pure exhaustion. She'd hardly slept over the past two days, replaying in her mind over and over what she'd seen out in the woods. First, her sister lying on the ground, not breathing. Then, seeing Susan transformed into some sort of creature. Deep in the back of her mind, she could look past her denial to see the truth. The truth that whatever was wrong with Susan, there was no coming back. The same truth that she'd fought to ignore over the last couple of days.

When her mother started to cry harder, a kind of guilt poured over Mary Beth. She knew that none of this was easy on her parents, and the decision to leave Susan behind couldn't have been easy. She came out of her ball, wiped her eyes, and stood.

"I'll go pack a bag."

***

The Dawsons lived a few miles away from the main roads. Mary Beth looked out the windows to see the same, ranch-style houses that she'd seen hundreds of times before when heading into town. She sat in the back seat, hugging her duffle bag in her lap. Her father had advised her to pack light and only bring necessities, which ended up just being clothes and toiletries. She'd left room in her bag for Bun-Bun, a purple stuffed bunny her grandmother had given her and that she'd had for as long as she could remember, as well as a small keepsake that Susan had knitted for her which had the letters "MBD" sewn into the corner. Each of her parents had also brought only one bag, and they'd filled up two others with dried and canned foods, as well as various bottles and jars filled with water.

They reached the main road of town. To her right was the grocery store that Mary Beth had been to with her mother more times than she could count. A mile off to the left was highway 129, the road they'd be taking to Knoxville. None of the businesses appeared to be open, even though it was well into the morning. Across the street, the windows of the gas station had been completely shattered. Mary Beth squinted her eyes into focus to see the inside of the convenience store trashed. Cars lined the streets, facing different directions. Other stores lining the street looked similarly vandalized.

"What the hell happened?" her mother asked.

Her father let off the brake, and eased the vehicle out onto Main. He drove at a snail's pace as they each scanned the area outside, trying to take everything in. To Mary Beth, it was as if a tornado had blown through town, leaving behind nothing but pure devastation.

"Look, honey, a person," Mary Beth's mother said, pointing just ahead. "Pull up and ask them if they know anything."

The person walked in the middle of the road, their back turned to the Dawsons. The figure moved with a limp and bad posture. Mary Beth noticed the tattered clothes. He appeared to be a man.

"I think he needs help," her mother said.

The man stopped, and her father hit the brakes. He put the gear into park and unfastened his seatbelt.

"I'll be right back," her father said.

Mary Beth's mother grabbed his arm. "Where are you going? Just pull the car beside him."

"I'm just gonna see if he needs help."

Her father opened the door and stepped out of the car.

He'd come within a few feet of the man when he stopped and said, "Jesus, are you okay?"

The man turned, let out a spitting snarl, and lunged at Mary Beth's father. Both her and her mother screamed, watching her father just miss the man's grasp. The man fell to the ground, and her father bolted back to the car.

Mary Beth looked into the man's eyes as he worked himself back up to his feet. Pale and empty, just like Susan's. His skin was further decayed and rotted than hers had been, though. He looked like a monster, not a human.

"Go, go!" her mother shouted.

Mary Beth and her mother simultaneously screamed as her father drove the vehicle right at the man. After a crash, Mary Beth looked up, and saw the windshield wipers clearing blood off the glass.

"I just clipped him. The car's fine," her father said.

"Are you okay?" The voice came from her mother, and Mary Beth looked up to see her looking into the back seat.

Mary Beth nodded.

"Put your seatbelt on," her father said, looking into the rearview mirror.

Mary Beth moved from the middle of the bench seat, and locked herself in behind her mother.

Her father veered onto 129, barely slowing down to make the turn.

***

Somewhere between Maryville and Knoxville was where Mary Beth's life changed forever.

She looked ahead, the city of Knoxville still far out of sight, and saw a woman and a child standing beside a truck on the side of the road, the woman waving her arms frantically.

"They need help, Charles," Maria said.

Mary Beth's father looked straight ahead, his hands tightly gripping the wheel. He failed to acknowledge what her mother had said.

"Are you going to stop? It doesn't look like any of the sick people are around." her mother noted.

"No," her father replied, short and to the point.

As they passed by the woman and the child, the freckled boy locked eyes with Mary Beth. When she looked back, the boy held her gaze, and Mary Beth saw the desperate look in the woman's face.

"How can you just leave them?" her mother asked. "She had a child, dammit."

"Yeah, and so do we," her father said, raising his voice. "Do you want me to get us to safety, or have you already forgotten what happened to Susan?"

Mary Beth's mouth fell open in surprise, and she noticed the instant regret in her father's face.

His lips moved, obviously trying to spew out words, and he finally bumbled out, "Honey, I'm sorry, I didn't mean to—"

"Don't try to backpedal," her mother said. "You said it." She drew in a deep breath. "Just keep driving."

But Mary Beth's father had already pressed the brake and cut the wheel toward the median. He found a gravel emergency vehicle path and used it to cross over to the southbound side of the highway.

The woman seemed to know that he had turned the vehicle around to come and assist her and her child, and she jumped up and down, yelling.

Mary Beth's father crossed back over the median and pulled up next to the truck.

"Oh my Lord, thank you," the woman said. She spoke in a very country accent that reminded Mary Beth of one of her uncles, who lived somewhere out in the middle of nowhere in Kentucky.

Her mother's window rolled down and her father leaned over to look out at the woman.

"Truck broke down?"

"Yes, sir," the woman replied. "Me and my boy here seem to be stuck."

"Do you need a ride into town?" he asked.

The woman shook her head. "I think it's an easy fix, I just don't have no knowledge 'bout cars. You don't by chance know somethin', do ya?"

"A thing or two," her father replied.

He undid his seatbelt and opened the door.

"Be careful," her mother said.

Mary Beth's father looked back to her mother and smiled before stepping out of the vehicle. He moved around the front and stopped at the hood of the woman's truck. It had already been raised and propped open.

Mary Beth watched her dad duck his head under the hood, and then her eyes were drawn to the boy's. He looked to be around her age, and something struck her as funny about him.

Unlike her, he didn't appear to be scared. Even his mom had been scared, so how could he look so calm? He smiled at Mary Beth. Not the kind of smile that a boy from school had once given her where his face had turned red before he looked away. This was something scary, something strange.

"Mommy," Mary Beth said. "Mommy, I'm scared."

Her mother looked into the back seat and smiled at her daughter. "I know, sweetie. So am I. But everything is going to be fine."

A loud crash and a scream drew Mary Beth's attention outside, and her mother turned back, as well.

"Oh my God, Charles!"

Her father lay motionless on the engine. A man towered over him, holding the truck's hood in his hand. He pushed it all the way up, then slammed it down onto Mary Beth's father again. A grotesque *crack* sounded through the air, and her father's limp body slid down the front of the truck, onto the ground. Mary Beth's scream harmonized with her mother's.

Panting, her mother jumped over the center console, into the front seat. When she went to shut the door, another man appeared, holding it open.

"No!" Mary Beth's mother cried.

Laughing, the man reached in and pulled Mary Beth's mother out of the vehicle. Mary Beth cowered into the corner of the back seat as her mother's kicking legs disappeared and her scream moved into the open air. Tears flowed down Mary Beth's face, and she felt a sudden sense of vulnerability; a type of fear that she'd never realized.

Bang.

The loud noise startled Mary Beth and she sat straight up.

Her mother screamed, "No!"

Mary Beth looked to the front of the truck and saw one of the men aiming a gun at the ground. Her eyes moved down to see the quivering legs on the asphalt. Her father's legs.

Bang.

The man had pulled the trigger again, and her father's legs had stopped moving.

"Daddy?" Mary Beth whispered.

Her mother continued to wail, looking back toward Mary Beth. She urged the people to leave them alone. But moments later, she was out of view, taken to the other side of the truck. Mary Beth heard her mother cry out, followed by a loud 'thump'.

Bang.

Her mother stopped screaming.

Then the car door opened, and the woman, laughing hysterically, stuffed a sock into Mary Beth's mouth and blindfolded her. Mary Beth bit down on the sock, trying to scream out, before she was picked up, and tossed into the stiff metal bed of the truck.

The engine, apparently working just fine, roared to life, and the truck pulled away.

Mary Beth never got the chance to confirm with her own eyes whether her parents were alive or dead. Instead, the terrifying people who'd abducted her dragged her off to a farm where she was sure she'd spend her final days.

CHAPTER SIX

Mary Beth's story left a dark cloud looming inside of the van. No one spoke.

The story made Gabriel think of Katie and Sarah. As scared as Mary Beth and her mother had been at the moment when their world had been turned upside down by this demonic plague, at least Mary Beth's father had been there for them. He was confident that Katie would put Sarah first and make sure that she was safe, of course, but he also knew the way Katie typically handled stressful situations. Many times, she would overreact before thinking things through. He should have been there. His palms sweating, he gripped the leather-covered steering wheel tight. The further toward the coast the group drove, the more anxious Gabriel became. And though they were making progress toward him getting home, he still felt so far away.

The voice next to him broke him away from his thoughts.

"You want me to drive?" Jessica asked. "You drove all day yesterday."

Gabriel shook his head. "I'm fine. I prefer this."

"How're we doing on gas?" Will asked from the back seat.

Gabriel chewed on his bottom lip. Though he needed to keep close attention to it, the gas gauge only stressed him out. He'd chosen to ignore it, much like people ignore the need for going to the dentist. The last thing he wanted was to have to waste time finding another vehicle on the road that met the list of criteria the group had; it had to start, be spacious enough for five people and their things, and have plenty of gas. It wasn't exactly ideal to have such a wish list with the threat of flesh-eating creatures wandering around outside.

"The light's been on for a few minutes now," Jessica said, replying to Will's question for Gabriel.

Everyone fell silent.

They'd all grown accustomed to ignoring the Empties outside. Even the children didn't let the beasts faze them anymore. But with Jessica's answer to Will, each person in the van became acutely aware of the danger lurking outside.

In an attempt to ease the mood, Gabriel reached down and powered on the stereo. Inside, the same The Cadillac Three CD that they'd heard many times over the past few days spun to life. Though Southern rock wasn't Gabriel's favorite, hearing the music play was a welcome alternative to the snarling beasts outside.

As they passed over the top of a steep Appalachian incline, Gabriel's eyes widened.

"My God," Jessica said from the passenger seat.

Smoke rose from a building a few miles further up the open road. They weren't coming into a city, but a small town along the I-40 countryside. A building sat aflame, and from what he could see, it didn't appear that any emergency crews were there fighting it off.

As they approached, Gabriel noticed something. A sign of hope.

Another mile up the road, he took the exit.

***

Gabriel pulled the van into the parking lot of Home Depot. The burning building sat about a block away. He pulled to the front of the store and shifted the van into park. The glass front doors and windows had been shattered, the place apparently already ransacked by looters.

"I don't see any Empties anywhere," Holly said.

"They may have been attracted to the fire," Will suggested.

"Doesn't mean there won't be some inside," Jessica said.

Gabriel unfastened his seatbelt and turned back to the group. "We need to go inside and see if we can find some gas cans and a hose," he said. "Though, I doubt we'll have much luck."

"I'll go in with you," Will said.

Gabriel nodded, then looked over to Jessica. "When I get out, jump into the driver's seat. Keep it cranked, because it's gonna use more gas turning the engine back over if you shut it off."

"You three keep a look out the back and sides for her," Will said to Holly and the two children. "Can you do that, kids?"

In near unison, the children nodded.

Will looked to Gabriel. "You got ammo for your pistol?"

"I'm good. Just grab that rifle for me."

Will reached into the bag and retrieved ammunition for his own sidearm. He then grabbed the rifle for Gabriel and a shotgun for himself, and moved to get out of the van. A hand squeezed his arm.

"If you aren't back in ten minutes, I'm coming in after you," Holly said, looking back at Will and holding onto his forearm.

Will smiled and said, "I'll be back." He leaned over and kissed Holly. "I promise."

***

Shards of glass lay all over the entrance, covering three human bodies, the flesh on them having been picked apart. Every display in sight had been turned over and emptied. At first glance, only useless items seemed to have been left behind. Looters apparently had no interest in planting flowers, as packs of daisy and lily seeds covered the ground near the customer service desk to their left.

"It looks like a tornado rolled through this place," Gabriel said.

"Strange we haven't seen anyone around. You'd think with as much shit that's gone that we would've seen more people," Will said.

"Maybe they all retreated back into the mountains."

Will chuckled. "If they're smart."

Gabriel looked over to the right and saw the entrance to the garden center.

"Come on," he said, and he stepped over an empty display rack to begin making his way to the outdoor area.

They moved with caution, listening for the snarls of the beasts, or even the murmurs of humans. So far, they'd heard nothing but their own steady footsteps and breaths. They reached the entrance to the garden center and moved to the fenced-in, outdoor area.

To no surprise, most of this section had been left alone. The middle of the space was filled with concrete fountains, yard gnomes, and flowers. The displays all seemed to be in tact.

"Doesn't look like this place has been touched," Gabriel said.

"Might get lucky and find a hose out here."

Gabriel turned when he heard a strange noise, and saw far across the room a shape lumbering along the edge. He put his arm around Will and threw them both down to the ground.

"Shit," Will said, and Gabriel put his finger up to his mouth.

"I saw something over there," Gabriel whispered, pointing across the large, open enclosure. "Over there where those few aisles of racking are, I saw something moving. I think it was an Empty."

"Toward or away from us?" Will asked.

"Away."

"Alright," Will said. "I'm gonna see if I can sneak around behind it. Go cut it off and be ready to get its attention. Hopefully, it's alone."

Will pushed up from his stomach and started down the perimeter of the room in a crouch. Gabriel got up onto one knee and crouched down behind a concrete garden fountain. He watched Will move to the wall on the other side of the large garden center, sneaking down one of the aisles. Will looked back to Gabriel, and gave him the signal to move.

Gabriel stood and jogged through the middle of the room, being sure to keep low and mostly hidden out of sight.

The last aisle came into view, and the figure appeared. It was, indeed, an Empty. It wore the patented orange apron of an employee, and hissed when it caught sight of Gabriel. Plenty of distance separated Gabriel from the Empty, and he figured he wouldn't have to move too close before Will came up behind the thing and took care of it.

"Over here, you ugly piece of shit!" Gabriel shouted. "Think you can show me where the hoses are?" He laughed.

The beast snarled.

Gabriel turned, pointing the rifle toward the main part of the store when he heard a scream. Not the snarl of a beast, but the distinct cry of a person. He heard quick footsteps and saw a flash in his peripheral of someone running toward the scream.

It was Will.

"Will!"

CHAPTER SEVEN

Jessica sat with her hands firmly on the steering wheel. A handgun sat in the seat beside her, loaded and ready in case any threat showed up around them. She peeked into the rearview mirror and saw the two children doing their part to help, Dylan looking out his side of the van, Mary Beth looking out of hers. Holly sat in between the two children, checking outside the rear window. Not wanting to scare the children any further, she didn't hold a gun, but she had a slew of them in the seat behind her. The two women caught each other's gazes when Holly looked into the front seat.

"How long's it been?" Holly asked.

"Almost ten minutes," Jessica said.

Holly let out a deep sigh.

"Just give them a little time," Jessica said. "It's a big store."

Jessica froze when she heard a noise. It sounded like it may have come from the inside of the store. Her face was blank of any emotion, giving off the signal that something concerned her.

"What?" Holly asked.

Jessica could have sworn the noise she'd heard was a scream, but Holly didn't seem to have heard it. And to tell Holly about it would only make her run recklessly into the building, doing so all on a hunch.

"Nothing," Jessica said.

***

Gabriel stopped just outside the garden center when he heard the scream again. This time, it came with a word.

"Help!"

It was a man's voice, and it sounded as if it were coming from the back of the store.

Gabriel raced down the paint aisle. He was forced to dodge cans and hop over puddles of spilled paint on the floor, but he managed to get through without slipping and falling.

He'd arrived across from the appliances section when he reached the end of the paint aisle, and stopped to look both ways to see if he could see Will, the man who was screaming, or any Empties.

A snarl and another scream.

A gunshot. Then another.

Shit.

Gabriel turned and followed the sound.

Two more gunshots.

He jogged down the center lane in the back of the store, glancing down each aisle to his right and left as he passed them.

As he came to the plumbing area, he looked down the aisle to his right. Displayed on the walls on either side were water faucets and various sink parts. In the middle of the aisle, four bodies lay sprawling. Blood soaked the floor. Will stood in the middle of the aisle, his shotgun in hand, trying to calm a man down.

"Will," Gabriel said, and he hurried over.

Gabriel looked down to the bodies as he passed them. Three of them were women and one was a male — all of them Empty. The man and one of the women wore the same orange aprons as the Empty in the garden center had sported.

"You alright?" Gabriel asked Will.

Will nodded.

Gabriel turned his attention to the stranger in the red t-shirt and dark jeans, who had his hand over his heart, trying to catch his breath. He was black, and looked to be in his late 30s or early 40s.

"Thanks so much, man," the guy said. "Holy shit." He ran both his hands through his short afro and said, "My name's Charlie Luck."

"Luck? No shit," Will said, taking the man's hand and smiling. "I'm Will Kessler."

Gabriel stuck out his hand. "Gabriel Alexander."

"Good to meet you gentlemen," Charlie said. "Where you from?"

"All over," Will said. "We all kinda met in Nashville, and now we're headed to D.C. That's where Gabriel's from and where his family is."

"I see. Any contact with them?"

Gabriel shook his head.

"Sorry, man," Charlie said. "What are you guys doing here?"

"Been having trouble finding gas," Will replied. "We came in here hoping to find a hose and maybe a gas can or two."

"Definitely not gonna find any cans," Charlie said. "Those've been gone a while."

"You've been here?" Gabriel asked.

Charlie nodded. "Many times."

Gabriel turned, readying the rifle to his shoulder, when he heard approaching footsteps.

"It's just me," Holly said.

She showed her face around the corner of the aisle's end cap. Holly's eyes widened when she looked to the floor and saw the bodies, and then she hurried over to Will.

"You okay?" Holly asked him.

"Fine. Where's Jessica and the kids?"

"In the van, keeping an eye on things."

While Will explained to Holly what had happened, Charlie turned and stepped around the back corner of the aisle. When he reappeared, he wore a jacket and was adjusting the collar. Gabriel pushed past Will. Charlie looked up just as Gabriel approached him, and he opened his eyes wide and raised his eyebrows. Gabriel grabbed Charlie by the collar and slammed him against a display of faucet parts.

"What the fuck, man?" Charlie said.

"Gabriel!" Will yelled.

"Where'd you get that jacket?" Gabriel asked.

"What?" Charlie asked, face painted with confusion.

Together, Will and Jessica worked to pry Gabriel away from Charlie, who lost his balance and fell onto the ground. He stumbled to his feet again and backed away.

"Let me go," Gabriel demanded. "He's wearing my fucking jacket!"

The blue ski jacket looked identical to the one he'd grabbed at the sporting goods store right after The Fall.

"You're crazy, man," Charlie said. "This is my jacket. It was a Christmas gift."

"Let it go, Gabriel," Holly said. "That's a common jacket."

Gabriel didn't buy the lie. "Take it off and show me the tag."

"What?"

Gabriel drew his sidearm and pointed it at Charlie, who put his hands up and moved backward away from the group.

"Gabriel, chill out," Will said.

"What the fuck?" Charlie said.

"Quit backing up," Gabriel said. "Pull off the jacket and show me the tag. If it's my jacket, it won't be there because it got ripped off in a struggle with an Empty. That whole part of the inside is torn."

Sweat pouring down his face, Charlie said, "Come on, man. I told you, this was a Christmas gift from my mother."

"Show me the tag," Gabriel said, shaking the weapon at Charlie. "I'm not gonna ask you again."

"Charlie?" a female voice called out.

Will and Holly raised their weapons, aiming them in the direction of the new voice.

"Who is that?" Will asked.

A woman appeared at the end of the aisle, and she drew her own gun, holding it up in front of her face and pointing it at Gabriel. She didn't have a clear shot with Charlie standing between them, and Gabriel quickly grabbed Charlie, turned him toward the woman, and held the handgun affixed to Charlie's temple.

"Drop it," Gabriel demanded.

Hands shaking, the woman continued pointing the gun at the group.

"Drop it, now, or he's done."

His voice shaking, Charlie said, "Do it, Claire."

Claire's hands continued to shake. She looked to be in her mid to late twenties, around the same age as Jessica and Holly. She looked more than uncomfortable holding a gun.

"Do it!" Charlie said once more, and the girl finally kneeled down and placed the gun on the ground.

"Kick it over here," Gabriel said.

Claire kicked the gun, sending it floating over the tile floor. It landed just to Gabriel's right, and Holly kneeled down to pick it up.

With Charlie his captive and Claire unarmed, Gabriel pulled at the back of the jacket collar and smiled. He leaned out of the way so the rest of his group could see that the jacket had been torn where the tag should've been, just like he'd said. Will's face turned from feeling confusion over how they'd got into this situation to anger. He pulled Charlie away from Gabriel, pushed him against the display wall, and punched him square in the jaw. Charlie crumbled to the ground and Claire cried out.

"Is it just you two?" Will asked Charlie.

"Y-yes," Charlie replied.

Will drew his own sidearm, pointed it down at Charlie's head, and asked again.

"Yes, I promise!" Charlie cried.

Gabriel kept a steady aim on the woman, watching to make sure she didn't do anything rash, while Will put away his gun, reached down, and picked up Charlie. He grabbed Charlie's shoulders and yanked the jacket off of him, then threw it back to Gabriel. Will then looked back to the rest of the group.

"Come on, let's go," he said.

"That's it?" Gabriel asked. "They know the vehicle we're in and everything."

"They're not gonna come after us," Will said.

"How can you be so sure?" Gabriel asked, keeping his gun aimed at Claire.

"Come on," Will said again.

Gabriel peeked over his shoulder to see Will walking away, and then he looked back to Charlie. Charlie had his eyes on Will and said, "Wait."

Gabriel looked back again to see that Will had stopped and turned to face Charlie. Gabriel followed his gaze back to the cowering man on the floor, waiting for him to speak.

"You saved my life," Charlie said. "I would've been eaten by those things if you hadn't showed up."

"Consider it a goodwill gesture," Will said.

"Let me pay you back," Charlie said.

Gabriel narrowed his eyes. "How, and *why* the fuck would you do that?"

Charlie looked down to the ground and shook his head. "Look, man, I'm sorry that I broke into y'all's van and stole your jacket and gasoline. We're just out here trying to survive like y'all are. You gotta understand that."

"Yeah," Gabriel said. "That's why we're leaving."

Gabriel lowered the gun and turned around. He nodded to Will, signaling to him that he was right in saying they needed to go try to find a hose and then get out of there.

"We have gasoline," Charlie said.

Gabriel immediately looked to Will and shook his head. Will's eyes moved back and forth between Gabriel and Charlie.

"Where?" Will asked.

"About twenty minutes from here," Charlie said. "We have a place up in the mountains. None of these monsters are up there."

Gabriel laughed, "What? So we're just supposed to follow you up into the middle of nowhere and expect you're just gonna give us some gasoline?"

When he looked back to Will and Holly, neither of them were laughing.

"I owe you guys my life," Charlie said. "We're good people up there, and we don't mean you any harm. We're just trying to survive this mess, just like y'all."

"How much can you give us?" Will asked.

Gabriel scoffed and said, "You're not really considering this, are you?"

Will pulled Gabriel aside, out of earshot of both Charlie and

Claire.

"Look, I've got a pretty good read on people," Will said. "They aren't a threat to us. I saw it in his eyes when I saved him. Just trust me on this one, okay?"

To Gabriel, none of this felt right. He simply wanted to get the fuck out of there and get on with their business. All he cared about was getting to his wife and kid, and he could give two shits about either of these people or their group up in the mountains. But when he looked into the face of not only Will, but Holly, as well, he knew he'd be fighting a battle he wouldn't win. So, instead of throwing a verbal jab, he simply sighed.

"We go there, we get gas, and we leave," Gabriel said. "Cool?"

Will nodded. "Cool."

He patted Gabriel on the shoulder, then turned back to Charlie and Claire.

"So, where exactly is this place you speak of?"

CHAPTER EIGHT

Will followed Charlie and Claire through the exit located at the rear of the store. Outside, Charlie and Claire's four-door sedan sat nearly blocking the back door, giving the door just enough room to swing open. The vehicle looked to be in less-than-stellar condition, the right side of the front end bashed in.

"I think you guys need a new car," Will said.

Claire said, "We've got others at camp. We just use this one for runs since it's already beat-up."

"How many times have you guys made this trip down here?" Will asked.

"Too many to count," Charlie said. "This is a small town, and it's gotten easier and easier to come down here because less people have been around. Not really sure if they're staying in their homes or... well..."

"Yeah," Will said, not needing Charlie to finish the sentence. He assumed the latter, unsaid notion that people were either not surviving, or worse, being possessed by the Empties.

An engine hummed at the far corner of the building, and Will looked over to see the minivan coming toward them. Gabriel brought the van to a stop a car-length away from the sedan's front bumper, and then he and Holly stepped out of the front seat. Jessica remained in the middle row with the kids.

"How far you say this place we're going is?" Gabriel asked.

"We're gonna go east down the interstate for about five miles, then we'll have a twenty minute hike up into those mountains over there," Charlie said, pointing out to the horizon.

Gabriel scoffed. "Well, I can tell you right now that we're not gonna make it up any mountains. We'd be lucky to get that five miles down the interstate on the fuel we've got in the tank."

From the driver's side of the sedan, Charlie smiled, hinged over on one foot, and popped the trunk. He walked around to the back of the car, reached into the trunk, and pulled out a five gallon gas can.

"This one should have enough inside to get you where we're going," Charlie said. He offered the gas can to Gabriel.

Hesitance in his eyes, Gabriel slowly put his hands out to take the gas can.

"Thanks," Gabriel mumbled.

"No problem, man," Charlie said.

Will walked to the passenger side panel door of the van and slid it open. He pulled out the handgun they'd taken from Claire, and handed it over to Jessica.

"You mind putting that back there for now?" Will asked.

Jessica reached back and placed the gun into one of the duffle bags.

"You need anymore ammo for yours?" she asked, looking back while still leaning over the seat.

"I should be good," Will said, shaking his head.

He felt a presence behind him and turned to see Holly.

"I wanna ride with you," she said.

"You need to stay with the others in the van. Besides, I don't think they have room for me in that car, much less two of us."

"Why can't you just ride with us, too?" Holly asked. "I'm with you, I'm not getting bad vibes from them, but you never know. Just ride with us and we can all just follow them up there."

"That's why I want to ride with them. If I get the sense that something isn't right, I can do something to get us out of it before they get us all the way up that mountain. But I think we're going to be fine."

Her eyes faced down, signaling to him that she still felt uneasy. He cupped her face in his hands and leaned in to kiss her on the forehead.

"Trust me," Will said. "It'll be fine."

***

Charlie merged onto Interstate 40 and headed east. Claire rode in the passenger seat and Will sat in the back, his sidearm neatly tucked away at his side. The sun sat in the sky, bringing with it a midday's heat. Grey clouds shifted in the distance, hinting at rain.

"Gotta think these warm days'll be past us soon," Charlie said, striking up friendly conversation.

"I'm lucky if I even know what month it is at this point," Will said.

"Some of the others in our group keep a calendar up-to-date, but I try not to look. It's not as if it really matters."

Will smiled. Time to him seemed so futile now. He'd thought he'd have plenty more holidays with his parents, and that they'd be around when he finally decided to settle down and get married, and even have a child. But none of that would happen now, and time seemed not to matter much to him, either. In fact, time was bullshit.

"How many are in your group?" Will asked.

"Including Claire and I, there's seven of us now."

The *now* definitely caught Will's attention, and the next logical question of wondering what happened to the others nearly came spewing out of his mouth. He caught himself, though, knowing that either Charlie or Claire would prod right back if he chose to question how many people they'd had in their group to begin with. Will wasn't ready to give his own answer back, in hopes that it could maybe come up later for Gabriel, Holly, or Jessica to answer.

Instead, Claire came at Will with another question he wasn't ready to give a direct answer to.

She asked, "Any idea what in the world caused all this?"

Will chewed on the question for a moment, thinking carefully how he'd answer. He even found himself involuntarily pulling away his shirt sleeve and massaging the bite marks on his arm, before realizing what he was doing and quickly pulling the sleeve back down to his wrist.

"I don't know," Will said, lying.

"Gotta be some kind of virus," Charlie said. "At least, that's what we think. One of the guys with us is hellbent on thinking that it's a biological terrorist attack, like ISIS or something. Like maybe someone contaminated our food or water system somehow."

"Terrorist attack," Will said. He nodded in agreement and said, "Makes a lot of sense."

And in a way, it really did. Only Will knew that ISIS wasn't behind the attack, but that instead it was some sort of supernatural being.

"So is that why you're headed to D.C.?" Claire asked. "To see if they have any answers there?"

"Kinda," Will said. "We're mainly going because that's where Gabriel and Dylan are from. Gabriel's the one who wanted to shoot Charlie."

A nervous laugh came from Charlie. "Yeah, well, glad he didn't. That his son?"

"Dylan? No. They were in a plane when The Fall happened. It crashed. They were the only two survivors."

"Damn," Claire said. "They survived a plane crash?"

Will nodded.

"You said 'The Fall'," Charlie said. "What do you mean?"

"Yeah, that's what we call it. I was sleeping when it happened, but apparently everyone who was initially infected just randomly fell to the ground. So, we started referring to it as 'The Fall' in our group."

Charlie had enough awareness to turn on his turn signal before exiting off the interstate, or perhaps it was just an old habit he'd held onto. Will looked outside and saw the sign that said 'Campgrounds' and had an arrow pointing to the left, the same direction that Charlie headed at the end of the ramp, again applying his turn signal as a courteous gesture to Gabriel, still driving the van behind them.

Cars were vacant, scattered across the bridge. A truck had even driven into the concrete barrier, its front tires now hanging off the edge, looking down onto Interstate 40. Will had one of those rare moments where he reminded himself that each one of the vehicles he saw along the road represented a life. He'd put himself past thinking about such things, but occasionally the thought snuck up on him. And for just a moment, he wondered if the person who'd been driving the truck had wrecked because they fell Empty, or wrecked in sheer confusion at the chaos around them.

Charlie navigated through the vehicles as if he could have done it with his eyes shut, and about another mile down the road, he pointed to a large billboard.

"That's where we're headed."

The billboard showed your typical asshole American family, complete with a happy husband and wife, a son and a daughter — all white, of course — and a yellow Labrador Retriever. The parents stood in an embrace on the front porch of a log cabin, looking out into the yard as the two children played with Old Yeller, little Timmy rearing back to throw the dog a tennis ball. The top of the billboard read, in big yellow letters, 'Visit Point View Cabins - Where North Carolina Vacations'. The sign also informed those passing by that they were 15 miles out.

"Looks quaint," Will said.

Charlie chuckled. "Yeah, it might be just a little different than that now."

Will noticed how quiet Claire had been. Considering everything that had gone down in the store, he couldn't blame her for being unsure about him and his group.

"So, how do you two know each other?" Will asked. "Friends? Couple? Brother and sister?"

The last suggestion got a small laugh out of the two, considering Charlie's light chocolate skin and Claire's a-typical suburban white girl appearance, complete with the blonde hair and blue eyes.

"New friends," Claire said.

"So, you guys met after The Fall?" Will asked.

Charlie peeked at Will through the rearview mirror, and replied with a very shortened, "Yes."

Pain lay behind those eyes in the mirror, and Will felt as if he might be stepping over the line, prying too much. Just like he didn't want them doing to him. Charlie clearly had his own newly acquired memories that he was trying to block out.

"Sorry," Will said. "Wasn't trying to get too personal."

Charlie sighed and ran his hand through his hair. "No, it's okay, man."

Claire reached over and rubbed Charlie's shoulder, as he fought off tears.

"My," Charlie said, hesitating to start. He took a deep breath and started over. "I'd had the trip up here planned for months. It was supposed to be my wife and I's ten-year anniversary getaway. I'd saved all my PTO over the last year and a half for this trip." He stopped again to choke back tears.

"Man, you don't have to talk about this," Will said, feeling guilty that he'd ever even asked.

"Really," Charlie replied. "It's okay. I need to."

Will rubbed the scruff on his face and nodded at Charlie through the mirror.

"That morning, we'd decided to go hiking. That was the main reason we came up here. Desiree grew up in these parts and had done a lot of hiking as a kid. We're from Atlanta, and while it's a real active town, it's flat. Myself, I would have rather had gone to the beach, but I knew this is what D would have really wanted.

"Anyway, I got up and made her breakfast — french toast, her favorite. We sat out on the back porch of the cabin, sipping coffee, eating our weight in maple syrup and carbs, and looking out toward our mountain view. God, it was so beautiful. We spent a couple of hours just taking in the scenery. I work in I.T., so I sit in a cubicle most of the day and don't exactly get to see these kinds of things.

"After that, we drove ten miles or so to Rabbit's Run; it's this really difficult hiking trail. God forbid D just want to do something casual and relaxing. I remember, we reached—"

Charlie had to stop in order to gather himself. The tears really came now, and Claire rubbed his shoulder again.

"Do you want me to drive?" Claire asked.

Charlie shook his head. "I'm almost done."

He cleared his throat and continued.

"We hiked all the way to this waterfall. I'd never seen one in person, at least not like this. It scaled what had to be fifteen stories high. I just stood there next to her, basking in God's amazement and wonder. I wrapped my arm around my wife, and we put our heads together. Neither of us said anything; we just looked at the water comin' down and the mist it created.

"I smiled at her and turned around to leave. I said something to her, and at this point, I really don't remember what. All I remember is hearing the thud behind me and the splash in the water."

Charlie wiped his eyes and sniffled.

"When I turned back around to see what the noise was, Desiree was face-down in the water. I—"

Charlie bawled now. Nothing could keep him from crying his eyes out, and Claire hovered her hand over the steering wheel just in case Charlie had a lapse in judgement.

Will found himself at a loss for words.

"I'm so sorry, man."

Charlie sniffled and forced a smile into the mirror. He shrugged and said, "Hey, we've all lost somebody, right?"

Yeah, Will thought. *We have.*

CHAPTER NINE

As they rode up the steep incline, all that surrounded them were trees. Birds flew overhead, and Gabriel even had to slow the van once to avoid running over a rabbit. For at least a few moments, the world felt like the world again, as opposed to a playground for undead, evil spirits.

A sign off to the side of the road read: Point View Cabins - Just Ahead.

Gabriel had driven quietly for most of the trip. He'd remained uneasy about following these people up here. For one, he was getting tired of detours, regardless of how necessary they were. Add on to that the fact that they'd just held these two people at gunpoint, going as far as physically assaulting Charlie, and Gabriel stirred in his head the distinct possibility that they were headed straight into a trap. The one upside was that neither Charlie or Claire had a way to alert the rest of their group that they'd be coming, so some kind of surprise ambush was, more than likely, out of the question.

After a sharp turn, the cabins came into view. Dylan shot up in the back, leaning in between the front seats.

"That's where we're going?" he asked, a kind of excitement in his voice that Gabriel hadn't heard.

"That's where we're going," Gabriel replied, matter of fact.

"Cool!"

The place wasn't exactly what Gabriel had expected. When he and Katie had gone on a cabin vacation a few years ago in Vermont, they'd gone to a more remote location — a single cabin with a hot tub and a gorgeous view. This place was more like a campground. There were two rows of identical cabins, each with its own gravel pathway leading up to a short set of stairs connected to a small front porch. The cabins themselves looked big enough to only hold a small family in each one. It was the kinda place you'd come if you didn't want to spend a lot of money renting a place more secluded, especially if you planned on spending more time outside of the cabin than inside. The recreation area surrounding the cabins gave plenty of reason to be out in the open air. Picnic tables sat in the open, along with enough charcoal grills to make the entire area smell fabulous on a summer's evening. A few people who sat at the tables stood up, and appeared to be calling to others. This made Gabriel at least slightly anxious, and he took hold of the gun at his side.

As they approached the campground, Gabriel noticed something that finally took him away from the mirage of a vacation dreamland.

The blood.

Where the dirt ended and the dying grass began, the earth was blood-stained. He followed the trail off into the trees, where it became indistinguishable. There'd been a battle here, that much was certain.

The car in front of them veered right to a parking area where a collection of other vehicles sat. As Gabriel pulled forward and parked the van behind Charlie's car, the others in his group had all come outside and approached them. Gabriel noticed one of the men holding a rifle at his side, and he bit his lip. He looked to Jessica in the middle row of seats and said, "Grab a gun, now."

Gabriel unlocked the door and swung it open, his sweaty palm holding a firm grasp on his sidearm. Just as he was about to draw, Charlie cut the two groups off, facing the approaching people with his palms toward them.

"Hold up, guys," Charlie said. "Everything is cool, these are good people."

The group stopped, and the man, a handsome fellow in his mid-forties, nodded toward Gabriel.

"Why's he got his hand on a gun, then?"

"Why you pointing that rifle our way?" Gabriel spat back.

He felt a presence at his side and glanced into his peripheral to see Will approaching.

"Lay cool, man," Will said.

"You, too," Charlie said to his guy.

Gabriel stared at the man, who returned the favor. After a few moments, Gabriel finally gave in and released the grip on his gun. The other man did the same, letting the rifle slide around to his back, out of sight but still there, just in case. Claire appeared at his side and grabbed the man by the arm.

"It's cool, Thomas," she said. "They're alright."

Thomas looked up from Claire to Gabriel again, then gave a hesitant nod. Gabriel returned it.

Gabriel scanned the rest of the group standing before him. The chances that most of these people had known each other before The Fall seemed slim to none. The only ones who he guessed might have were an older couple, appearing to be in their 70s, standing on the outer edge of the group. There was a gangly-looking guy with a sad excuse for a beard on his face, likely in his early 20s, and a boy, probably slightly older than Mary Beth or Dylan, who rounded out the group.

Behind Gabriel, the other doors to the van opened, and Holly, Jessica, Mary Beth, and Dylan all exited.

Charlie turned to Gabriel and the others and smiled. "Let me introduce you to everyone."

He pointed to the older couple first. "This is Larry and Marie. They came up here for their 45th anniversary." The two smiled, and Larry waved to Gabriel and the others.

Charlie pointed to Sad Beard next. "This is Scott."

"Hey," Scott mumbled.

"This here is Reece," Charlie said, signaling to the young boy, who waved.

"And I'm Thomas."

Thomas approached Will and Gabriel, reaching his hand out. Gabriel accepted it, and the two men gripped each other's hands tight, in almost another battle of masculinity.

"Welcome," Thomas said. "If my sister says you're alright, then I guess that'll do." He looked back to Claire and smiled.

"You guys want to shower?" Charlie asked. "We've got well water up here."

"Yes," Holly said, raising her hand.

"Come on," Charlie said. "We'll show you guys around a bit."

***

At the far end of the campground sat a playground. Swings, slides, and monkey bars completed the set-up. It was separated from the woods by only twenty yards, meaning that the children had to be supervised by an adult, so Jessica and Scott stood watching for Empties while Dylan, Mary Beth, and even the slightly older boy, Reece, swung, slid, and hung on the monkey bars.

Gabriel looked on, happy to see Dylan being able to play with other children and act somewhat like a normal kid for a change. It brought a smile to his tired face as he sat with Will, Charlie, Thomas, and Claire. Holly had hurried to one of the cabins to shower, while the elderly couple of Larry and Marie had retreated to their own cabin for a nap.

"Sorry 'bout jumpin' your ass back there, man," Thomas said to Gabriel.

Gabriel chuckled. "It's alright. I wouldn't exactly say that I was Mr. Rogers back there."

"We all gotta stay on our toes with all the shit that's happened," Will said.

"So, why exactly y'all headed to D.C.?" Thomas asked.

"That's where me and the boy are from," Gabriel said, nodding toward Dylan, who was seeing how high he could get before jumping out of a swing. "He isn't mine, but I'm trying to get him home. I've got a little girl of my own and a wife I'm trying to get back to."

"Hmm," Thomas said, looking down at the rock he was tossing in his hand.

"What about you?" Will asked. "Where are you from, Thomas?"

"Really small town at the South Carolina-Georgia border called Hardeeville. It's just about a half hour drive from Hilton Head, and damn close to Savannah. I own a little auto garage down there. This was the first vacation I've taken that wasn't to the beach since I was a kid. Hardeeville's one of those places where everyone knows everyone, which means everybody thinks they're entitled to your business. Thought it'd be nice to get away."

"Worse places you could be stuck than up here," Gabriel said.

"Yeah," Thomas said, short and concise.

"So, there's seven of you now," Will said, "but how many of you were up here to begin with?"

There was an awkward pause. Thomas's face went pale in an instant. He rubbed his forehead. "Excuse me," he mumbled, pushing himself off the top of the picnic table and heading for one of the cabins.

Claire rubbed her eyes and looked to the rest of the group. "Sorry," she said, and she stood up from the picnic table and jogged after her brother.

"I'm sorry," Will said.

Charlie sighed and put his hand over his mouth, running it over the growing beard on his face and ending at his chin.

"This is the first time we've had other people up here," Charlie said. "We've been through a lot, ya know? A lot of shit went down up here."

Gabriel found it hard to believe that *anyone* had been through as much as Will since The Fall, and mentally commended Will on his restraint, to not reply with something sharp and cold.

"Maybe it'd be best if we just got what we came up here for and hit the road," Gabriel said.

"You don't want to stay for a little while?" Charlie asked.

Gabriel looked over to the playground. Dylan half-hung off a merry-go-round while Mary Beth and Reece stood on either side of it, spinning it around faster and faster. Dylan's hair blew in the wind, and Gabriel hadn't seen him smile like this at all in the short time that he'd known him. His heart sank with the reality that he'd have to pull the boy out of this, but knew it would happen sooner or later.

"We really need to get going," Gabriel said. "I think I can speak for all of us when I say that we appreciate your generosity and trusting us enough to bring us up here, especially with how things went down back at the store, but I should've been in Washington a week ago."

Charlie bowed his head and nodded. "Yeah, I understand."

Thunder sounded in the distance and Gabriel turned back to see dark clouds gathering in the sky. He looked up and could see the sun about to be overtaken by a gunmetal portrait directly above their heads. Within moments, the campground was overshadowed and Gabriel felt the first rain drop.

"Alright, we gotta get goin' so we don't get caught in this," Gabriel said.

Charlie chuckled. "The sky's about to open, man. You don't wanna be caught dead driving back down to the main roads in the rain, believe me. Especially in that minivan."

Gabriel sighed and started to speak again, but Will cut in.

"He's right," Will said. "We need to just wait this out up here."

A thunder clap roared in the sky again, and Jessica hurried over to the men gathered at the picnic table.

"Got somewhere we can go before it starts pouring?" she asked Charlie.

Charlie nodded. "I've got the keys to most these places in my cabin."

As Charlie hopped up off the picnic table and jogged to his cabin, Gabriel drew in a deep breath and shook his head.

"We need to get going. We can't waste anymore time."

"You kidding?" Jessica asked. "It's about to pour and we're in a minivan. We'll slide right off that road on the way down."

And then the sky opened.

CHAPTER TEN

Instead of all six of them cramming into one of the small cabins together, the group ended up in two units — Will, Holly, and Mary Beth in one. Two doors down, Gabriel, Jessica, and Dylan settled into another.

As rain pattered on the roof and beat against the gravel outside, Will looked around the living area of the small cabin. A half-empty water bottle sat on a coffee table next to an open entertainment magazine. In the small dining area, a jacket hung over one of the chairs pushed under the hand-built, wood table, large enough to seat six people.

Mary Beth and Holly appeared from a doorway on the other side of the room.

"Someone's clothes are on the bed," Mary Beth said. "Does someone live here?"

Will could see in Holly's face that she had figured out exactly the same thing he had. Someone *had* been staying here before the cabin suddenly became vacant.

"We'll check and see if they're Mr. Charlie's or one of the others' here, sweetie," Holly said, making up something to keep the child's head from spinning. "Why don't you go sit over there on the couch?"

Mary Beth skipped over to the loveseat and grabbed the magazine off the coffee table, rapidly thumbing through he pages to try and find something that interested her.

Will walked to the bedroom, grabbing Holly's arm to take her with him.

An open suitcase lay on the bed, a man's clothes neatly packed inside. On the floor at the other side of the bed lay another suitcase. It was closed, but a man's button-up plaid shirt lay on top of it, next to a pair of boots. The bed itself was unmade, its sheets and comforter tossed. Will walked to the bathroom and saw the toiletries neatly placed on either side of the twin vanity. He emerged from the restroom, coming to where Holly stood looking at the bed.

"This is just creepy," Holly said.

"I don't know," Will said. "When I was at the hospital, I lay in that bed wondering how many people had died in it."

"Yeah, but their crap wasn't still scattered all over the place."

Will looked to the side table and noticed an open condom wrapper on the ground. He narrowed his eyes and said, "Yeah, you've got a point."

Holly came over to him and wrapped her arms around him, nestling her head into his chest. After a few moments, she pulled away and looked up into his eyes.

"I did a lot of thinking while I was in the shower," she said.

There was an awkward silence, and finally Will said, "And?"

"I mean," she said, stumbling her words. "Do we really want to leave?"

Will furrowed his brow.

"Look at this place, Will. We've got everything we need up here. There's shelter, water, endless firewood. And Charlie said they haven't seen any Empties up here since after The Fall. It's almost like a sort of utopia. It's even better than the hospital."

Will nodded, not able to help himself but agree, but there was still the one big, obvious issue.

"Okay, but what about Gabriel?" Will asked.

"Did you see how happy Dylan was? You think he didn't

notice that?"

"Doesn't matter," Will said, shaking his head. "All that guy can think about is his wife and daughter. That's not to say he doesn't want Dylan to be happy, because he sure as hell cares for him. But he's not gonna stop until he gets home."

Holly looked toward the window, frustration in her face, then looked back up to Will. "You think they're alive?"

"Who?"

"His wife and daughter," Holly clarified.

Will allowed that question to just hang in the air. He let it sit long enough that, by the time he was ready to say something, a knock came at the front door. He put his hand on Holly's shoulder.

"You mind? It's probably just Gabriel or Jessica. I'll be there in just a sec."

"No problem." Holly left the room.

Will looked down at the suitcase on the bed and pulled out a navy blue long-sleeve tee. He opened it and sized it up in front of him. From the front of the cabin, he heard Charlie greeting Holly.

As Will walked over to the bathroom, he took off his shirt. He looked in the mirror and observed the various scratches on his body, not even sure at this point which had originated with which incident. Turning on the faucet, he leaned over and splashed water onto his face, rubbing away at the grime and dirt. When he picked his head back up, Charlie's face appeared in the mirror, standing in the room behind him. Will jumped.

"You scared the shit out of me."

Still wet from the pouring rain, Charlie smiled and chuckled. "Sorry, man."

Will grabbed a towel that felt dry and unused, and turned

around while drying his face. When he pulled the towel away, Will saw Charlie looking upon him with wide eyes. He was staring at the scratches and bruises on Will's chest before shifting his gaze to the swollen wounds on Will's arm.

"Holy shit," Charlie mumbled.

Will threw the shirt over his head and pulled it down, hiding all the marks. He glared at Charlie as he moved past him and out of the room.

"What's up?" Will asked, moving out to the living room. "Why'd you come over?"

"Just, uh, just checking in," Charlie said. "I brought you guys over some bread, peanut butter, and some mixed nuts."

"Thanks," Will said, sitting down at the dining room table. Holly and Mary Beth sat on the floor in front of the coffee table in the middle of the living room.

"I found a deck of Uno cards," Mary Beth said.

"Awesome," Will said, smiling.

"We've got some board games over in Scott's cabin," Charlie said. "He and Reece have been playing Monopoly and Clue a lot. I'm sure they'll let you play with them if you guys decide to stay long enough."

Will naturally turned to Holly, who was staring back at him. She smiled briefly, then looked back to the game, and Will knew they'd be finishing their conversation about the possibility of staying later on.

"Rain doesn't look like it's slowing down anytime soon," Charlie said. "Just wanted to let you know that you guys are welcome to stay the night if the day runs long and it's still a mess out there. You're gonna want that road nice and dry before you try to go down it."

"Thanks," Will said. Charlie was still exchanging a curious

look with him, and Will felt self-conscious about the bite wounds on his arm.

"Oh, and, uh, we've also got some firewood stocked away in one of the open cabins," Charlie said. "If you end up needing to stay here, you're welcome to use some for heat and light. It gets pretty chilly up here at night."

"Sounds good," Will said.

Charlie just stared at Will awkwardly for a moment, before turning down his gaze and grabbing his rain coat off the hook by the front door.

"Alright, well, I'll let you guys hang out and rest for a while. I'm over in cabin five if you need anything."

Will stood up and approached Charlie. He smiled and extended his hand, which Charlie grasped and shook.

"Thanks for everything, Charlie. We really appreciate it."

Charlie smiled. "No problem." He opened the door, and Will saw just how much rain was pouring down from the sky. "Talk to you soon."

***

The rain continued turning the dirt courtyard into mud as Gabriel watched out the window. With no power, the overcast sky made the inside of the cabin mostly dark. The sound of the shower running from inside blended in with the storm, as Jessica had been the first to go clean up when they came inside. Dylan lay on the sofa, tossing a ball into the air repeatedly and catching it, the rubber smacking his palm each time. Across the way, someone stepped out of one of the cabins, their head covered with a jacket, and ran across the courtyard. It was Thomas, and he appeared to be heading straight for Gabriel's cabin.

Gabriel sidestepped to the door and opened it, just as

Thomas' feet clattered up the four wooden stairs leading up to the cabin's front porch. He pushed the jacket off of his head.

"Mind if I come in?"

Gabriel shook his head and moved adjacent with the door, inviting Thomas inside. Thomas wiped his feet on the door mat lying just outside of the entrance, then came into the cabin.

"Not a bad set-up here, huh?" Thomas said.

Gabriel chuckled. "Have you been out there, out on the road? It could be a hell of a lot worse."

"Yeah, they could have put you in the place your friends are in. A couple of gay dudes were in there."

Gabriel chuckled and shook his head. "What brings you by?"

Thomas sighed. "Well, actually, I was just hoping that you and I could have a chat."

Gabriel furrowed his brow. "Yeah? Okay." He looked back to Dylan. "Hey, Dylan, why don't you run over to Will's and see what Mary Beth is up to?"

Dylan shot up off the couch and raced for the door.

"I thought you'd never ask," the boy said.

Gabriel caught him on the way by and said, "Whoa, whoa, make sure you go grab a coat so you don't get wet."

Dylan retreated to one of the bedrooms and returned with a coat on his back. It was the one Gabriel had grabbed for the boy at the sporting goods store at the same time he'd gotten his own. Gabriel reached down and pulled the hood over his head.

"Have fun," Gabriel said, and the boy was out the door, racing through the rain to the cabin two doors down.

Gabriel shut the door, and when he turned back around, Thomas had his hands on his hips and was staring out of a window above the sink. Not sure where this was headed, Gabriel crept into the kitchen, the wood floor creaking beneath his feet.

He made his way over to the dining room table, and shifted his weight onto the back of one of the chairs, rocking back and forth on his heels.

"So, what'd you wanna talk about?" Gabriel asked.

Continuing to watch the rain fall outside, Thomas didn't respond. Gabriel swallowed the silence.

"Um, Thom—"

"We'd looked forward to this trip for months," Thomas said, breaking his awkward silence. "I bought a special calendar which I put in my office at work just to mark down the days until we left to come up here. We were only coming for five days, which may not seem like a big deal to some people. But when you've worked as hard as I have to provide for your family, five days away from all the sweat, and coming home with hands stained black and bathed in the scent of motor oil; five days is a long fucking time."

There was another pause while Thomas cleared his throat and gathered himself. Footsteps approached from behind them and Gabriel turned to see Jessica emerge from the short hallway. She was drying her hair with a towel, wearing a white robe she must've found in a closet, and stopped dead in her tracks when she saw Thomas and Gabriel looking back.

"Oh, I'm sorry," Jessica said.

"It's alright," Thomas said. "I don't mind if you hear this."

Jessica stepped toward the sofa, continuing to pat her hair with the towel, and took a seat. She eyed Gabriel, as if to ask what was going on, and then Thomas continued.

"Probably 'bout an eighth of a mile through the woods, there's a water hole," Thomas said. "That's where Jake and I were when we heard the screams. My parents planned this trip about a month after Claire got divorced, and rented out three cabins for us. My dad was gonna come fishin' with me and Jake, but changed his mind at the last minute, opting instead to take a nap. It would've been weird enough if there had just been one scream, but this was several in unison. Jake and I left our fishing gear down by the water and ran as fast as we could back up here.

"When we arrived back at the campground, several people were outside. There was a lot of confusion. Claire stood in the middle of the group and ran to us when she saw us appear out of the woods. I asked her what was wrong, and all she could say was, 'Jane passed out! Jane passed out!' Jane's my wife, you see. I told Jake — my son, if you haven't figured that out by now — to stay outside with Claire, and I ran into the cabin.

"It was…"

Thomas paused again, this time because he'd started to cry. Gabriel, his face feeling hollow and pale, looked back to see Jessica wiping tears from her own eyes.

"The inside of the place smelled lovely. Jane and Claire had been baking and the kitchen counters were loaded with various cookies, a couple of pies, and they had a cake in the oven. The smell didn't match the feeling I had when I walked in the door. Then I looked over onto the kitchen floor and just saw a hand peeking out from the other side of a cabinet.

"I ran to her and kneeled down next to her. She was lying on her side, facing the cabinet, and I flipped her over. I'll never forget the eyes. They were wide open and lifeless. Deep down, I knew. She wasn't breathing, but I checked for a pulse anyway. When there wasn't one there, I began to administer CPR. As I'm sure you all know by now, it was useless. After that, I just lay there next to her, holding her hand at my lips and mumbling 'I'm sorry' over and over again, as if there would've been something I could've done if I'd been there.

"There were more screams outside, and I heard my sister call my name.

"When I ran outside again, I watched Miles, one of those queers who'd been staying in your friends' cabin, come walking across the picnic area out front toward the survivors. He had blood all around his mouth. He'd bitten his partner, you see? We found him later, all chewed up to hell. A fuckin' mess.

"I ran back into the house and grabbed my Remington. I always carry a sidearm, but we'd brought our deer huntin' gear with us, too. Glad we did.

"Before I even made it back outside, I heard more screams. When I made it back to the porch, I just couldn't believe what I was seeing. Miles was on top of a child — a little girl who'd belonged to a couple we later found out had become those monsters, as well. Some guy tried to get Miles off of her, but he got bit in the process. I ran over there, and I didn't know what else to do. I pulled out my handgun and shot him right in the head, without any hesitation."

"In hindsight, good on you for not waiting," Gabriel said.

Thomas nodded, then continued. "I turned around to look for Jake, but he wasn't there. I called his name, with no response. I knew there was only one place he would've gone."

"Oh, God," Jessica mumbled.

"I raced back to our cabin and hurried inside. Upon hearing me enter, Jake turned around to look at me. He was standing just outside the kitchen, where he could see his mother's body. He said to me, 'Dad, I think she's okay.' I was confused. Jane was dead, I knew it for sure. That's when I heard her make the sound. That grotesque, inhuman, sound."

Thomas looked up to the ceiling and drew in a long deep breath. He finally looked away from the window and turned to face Gabriel and Jessica.

"I tried to get him away, but it was too late. She bit right into Jake's calf. I watched my son fall to the floor in agony, and she was able to take a chunk out of the back of his neck before I finally pulled him away from her and carried him outside."

Gabriel looked to the ground, shaking his head. He brought his hand up to his face, covering his eyes.

"I shut the door behind me, and whatever my wife had turned into didn't have the sense to turn the knob and follow us outside. I laid Jake down onto one of those picnic tables outside, but there was so much commotion all around. More people had emerged from the cabins, transformed into those monsters. Two more people were on the ground being attacked. Everyone was yelling at me at once, seeing as I was armed. Honestly, I don't really remember much about what happened next. I left my son on the table and I just started shooting at any of the beasts. Everyone else ducked down and got out of the way. I slaughtered all the things that were out there. By the time it was over, Jake had stopped breathing, and he was gone.

"After that, I moved Jake into one of the cabins, shut the door, and then went outside to check on Claire. She was bawling, because she had discovered our parents had both turned, as well. Phones didn't work, and we just passed it off for bad reception up here, so I knew I'd have to go for help. I was about to jump in my truck and go find help when I heard the banging at the door of the cabin where I'd left Jake. He was—"

Thomas leaned over one of the chairs, bracing himself with one hand and covering his face with the other.

"I'm sorry," he said, waving toward Gabriel and Jessica.

"It's okay," Gabriel said. "You don't have to continue."

Thomas shook his head, then looked up. "All night, I just sat on the picnic table listening to my wife, my parents, and my son, bang on three separate doors. It was almost like some sort of demon inside of my head, screaming at me from every direction."

"Excuse me," Jessica said, and she left the room, hiding tears.

"For two days, they remained in those cabins," Thomas continued. "I didn't want to accept what had happened to them. But then I made a few runs with Charlie, and we saw just how bad things had gotten. Those creatures were everywhere. We even talked to a couple of other people who had already received word that there wasn't a cure. I called 'bullshit' at first, but the more we encountered these things, the more we realized it was probably right. And I just couldn't take another night of my family bashing against the doors."

Thomas drew in one more long breath. "That night, I made my sister and the others lock themselves in one of the cabins, and Charlie and I opened the doors one at a time and put them down." He cleared his throat. "When we were finished, we burned the bodies over there." He pointed to the far end of the campground.

"My God," Gabriel said. "Why didn't you just let others do it?"

"I wish that question had an answer, man," Thomas said. "For whatever reason, I just felt I had to be the one to do it."

"I couldn't have done all that," Gabriel said.

"And that's why I'm here telling you this," Thomas said.

Gabriel cocked his head and narrowed his eyes at Thomas.

"As soon as you leave here, you need to get to Washington as fast as you can," Thomas said. "Don't stop and don't let anyone hold you back. These people are your friends, but that's your family out there. If I had any hope at all that my family was alive, I'd stop at nothing to get to them. And if you get to them, and you find them in the same state my family was in, then God help you. But I hope that you don't have to do what I had to do."

Every muscle in Gabriel's body tensed, and he became so enthralled by what Thomas had just said to him that he almost forgot to breathe. He'd thought back over and over again to the last conversation he'd had with Katie on the phone, thankful that it had been pleasant. But it still wasn't enough to mask the issues they'd had going on at home. All this played into Gabriel's guilt, and if he reached home and found that his wife and daughter were either dead or turned, then he'd already decided to make sure he had one extra bullet for himself. God forbid he have to live through what Thomas had lived through.

And as if the two men were brothers or best friends from childhood, they embraced in the middle of the dining room, both of them crying.

CHAPTER ELEVEN

Later on that evening, the hosts set up a bonfire at the end of the campground, just on the other side the playground. This had apparently been the group's routine, as Will had noticed earlier a collection of rocks that formed a circle around the charred remains of the wood they'd burned the previous evening.

Even though the rain had let up, Will and the others had collectively decided to stay the evening. Being out on the road at night was dangerous as it was, but making it back down the mud-caked mountain in pitch black would pose to be even more treacherous. The circumstances had brought more frustration upon Gabriel, but Will had been able to drive some sense into him, knowing that trying to get back out on the road that night would've been suicide.

When Will emerged from the cabin, the sun had gone to sleep, and the moon sat in the sky, possibly just another day or two from revealing its entire face. The clouds had dissipated in spots, revealing pockets of stars. Crickets chirped, and leaves in the woods ruffled every now and then. The entire campground was dark except for the bright orange glow of the bonfire. Each person sat just off from the flames, which illuminated their faces. There was a chill in the air, just as Charlie had warned them about earlier. Will wondered, even with all the available wood to burn surrounding them, how the group would survive up here once the temperatures really started to drop. And furthermore, what were he and his own group going to do once the temperatures fell? They would be in Washington by then, but what if this refugee camp they were hoping to find there was nonexistent? Will shook the thought off as he headed down the front porch staircase and walked across the courtyard to join the others by the fire.

As he approached, he quickly noticed the absence of Gabriel and Thomas. Everyone else was there, sitting basically shoulder-to-shoulder with each other. The three kids had their own little area, and the older couple, Larry and Marie, looked like Siamese twins, cuddled up under a blanket together. Will glanced over to Jessica.

"Where's Gabriel?"

"He didn't want to come out here," Jessica said. "I think he just wanted some time alone."

"Same with Thomas," Charlie said. "He's back at his place. Maybe he'll join us in a little while. Gabriel, too, if he has a change of heart. Have a seat."

Holly had saved a place for Will to sit between both her and Jessica. Holly patted on the ground beside her, inviting Will to sit down. He moved around the circle and plopped down onto a blanket which covered the mud.

"You guys sit out here every night?" Will asked.

"It's just started to get cooler over the last few nights," Claire said. "We've been trying to save most of the wood we've gathered for when it gets *really* cold, but this has been some really good bonding time for us over the last couple of evenings."

"There's only so much you can do up here at night with no power," noted Scott, the twenty-something year old guy who'd barely spoken a word up until now.

"Do you guys plan to just stay up here?" Jessica asked.

Charlie, Claire, and Larry all nodded.

"Where else would we go?" Larry asked. "Me and the misses

aren't exactly built for travel, especially out there, from the way that Charlie, Claire, and Thomas have described it."

"We've only been into town and back," Charlie said. "How bad is it out there?"

Will looked down, grabbing a twig and twisting it in his hand. "Bad."

"You guys don't want to go out there," Holly said. "Trust us."

"We'd only thought about it a little," Charlie said. "I think mostly we'd just like to try and find some answers about what the hell is *really* going on. About what's causing this."

Will could feel the eyes of Jessica and Holly on him without even having to look up. He ran his hand under his sleeve and rubbed the wound on his arm again. He wasn't sure if these people would believe him or think he was crazy, but he felt, with all the hospitality they'd shown, that they at least deserved to know what he and the others knew.

So, he told them.

He began with the experimental Empty at the hospital, explaining to them how the hospital's survivors had run some test and been unable to find any trace of a virus or infection within it. He told them what he knew about how to kill the beasts, which they'd already found out on their own through trial and error. Then, Will drew in a deep breath as he prepared to drop the bomb on them.

"We think the reason for the reanimation is supernatural. Something... demonic."

Charlie looked upon Will with a blank stare. He cleared his throat. "Demonic?"

Will nodded.

"You mean... like those things are possessed by demons?" Marie asked.

The old man, Larry, chuckled. "And what on earth makes you think that?"

Holly put her hand on Will's shoulder and nodded at him, glancing down to his arm. Will sighed, then rolled up his shirt sleeve. He leaned in toward the light of the flames and put his arm out for everyone to see.

There was a collective gasp as everyone looked down at the bite marks on Will's arm; then they all seemed to turn their eyes up to Will's.

Charlie said, "You got bit?"

Again, Will just nodded.

"Don't worry," Holly said. "He's not infected."

"How can you be so sure?"

"Because I watched a man draw the demon out of him," Jessica said, breaking her silence.

The campground survivors looked at Will, their jaws dropped and eyes wide. They looked as if they didn't believe Jessica.

"It's true," Dylan said. "I was there, too."

Will explained all that he knew about what had happened. How he'd gotten into the car accident, then been bitten by a man they'd had a confrontation with, sparing himself the pain of explaining to them who David Ellis was. To the point, it was irrelevant. He moved on, speaking about how he'd been bitten, and then eventually blacked out. Not just blacked out, but passed on. Holly and Jessica listened just as intently, as this was the first time he'd spoken this in-depth about what it had felt like to have died. He had no recollection of being revived by Samuel, the preacher, but used Jessica's account that she'd shared with him after she'd witnessed the exorcism herself. By the end of it, both Holly and Jessica were in tears, which caused a chain reaction to the children, Claire, and the elderly couple.

Most of the rest of the evening was spent in silence, with the occasional question or comment coming in. Will felt emotionally drained. He sat by the fire with Jessica and Holly, both cuddled up with him on either shoulder. He felt relieved, having finally spoken out loud about having almost been turned. He wasn't really sure if the campground survivors believed him, nor did he give a shit. He knew it was the truth, and felt that they'd earned the right to at least know what he and the others knew. These were good people, and like Will and his group, they'd need every advantage possible in order to survive in this hellfire of a new world.

Will spent the rest of his time outside staring into the fire and reflecting on the last few weeks, trying to pick out as many positives as he could.

Then, after a time, he finally retreated back to his cabin to get some rest.

CHAPTER TWELVE

The sun peeked in through the window of the bedroom, coming in at just the right angle to shine on Gabriel's face. He slit his eyes open, groaning and turning away from the light as it blinded him. He wished he would've thought better to close those blinds before passing out the night before.

He looked to the bed next to him and saw Dylan curled up under the blankets. When Gabriel had gone to sleep the previous night, the boy had still been away with the others. Gabriel had decided not to join the group. Every second of his life lately had been spent around the others, and he needed some time to himself to try and decompress from all the anxiety surrounding their situation. The previous day's talk with Thomas had only added to Gabriel's eagerness to get home. It had made him much more stressed than he'd already been. So, instead of singing "Kumbaya" around the campfire with everyone, Gabriel had burned a couple of logs in the chimney and sat in the living room, on the sofa, relaxing and thinking about everything from the plane crash to the hospital. But he'd mostly thought of his wife and daughter.

Gabriel carefully peeled the sheets off of himself and swung his legs off the side of the bed. Dylan didn't move. He continued to breathe easy, hopefully off dreaming about something happy. The previous night, Gabriel had made sure he had all his things together for a quick departure this morning. He slipped on his pants and shirt, which he had laid out the previous night, picked up his shoes, and crept out of the room, careful not to wake the boy. He pulled the door shut behind him, and noticed that the door to Jessica's room was open. He glanced inside, only to see an empty bed with the sheets and comforter still neatly tucked under the pillows, up to the top of the mattress. It looked as if she might have slept somewhere else the night before, or perhaps she had just gotten an early start and was somewhere else, inside the cabin or outside.

He didn't find her around anywhere, and after putting on his shoes, he opened the front door of the cabin and stepped outside.

The morning was cool and calm. Somewhat to his surprise, nobody was in the courtyard, making him wonder if he was the first person to have awoken. Maybe Jessica had slept at Will and Holly's. He glanced over to their cabin, and decided to head over.

As he approached, he saw a note taped to the front door. He moved up the steps and squinted his eyes to try to start reading it. The wind blew, causing the piece of paper to wave, and Gabriel grabbed it to keep it still.

Ran an errand with Charlie and Scott. Be back soon. - WK

An ounce of sweat tickled Gabriel's cheek, and he snatched the note off the door and crumpled it up in his hands. His blood boiled.

Gabriel marched down the steps and stormed back to his cabin.

***

It had seemed like it'd been years since Jessica had done this. Since she'd sat down by a body of water and watched the sun rise. The house she grew up in had been located in a subdivision that had its own private pond. She'd spent many mornings sitting on a pier out there, writing in her notebook and watching the sunrise before heading to school. This morning, she'd walked through the wooded area on the other side of the cabins and followed a narrow, dirt path back to a small pond. She had, of course, carried a gun with her, but was thankful that the short journey and the time alone had been peaceful.

After days on the road and with all the hell she'd been through, she found herself becoming almost jealous of the survivors at the campground. They had it made up here. They had shelter, an endless supply of firewood, a remote location that would be difficult for the Empties to navigate to, and were only a short drive away from a small town where they could go and get the supplies they needed. The only downside was that, eventually, they'd likely rob the stores of anything useful to them, and that's assuming that no one else wiped it out first. They'd have to find another way to find food when that happened, but still seemed a way's away from that reality.

In addition to bringing a gun down to the water with her, Jessica had also brought the notebook which Sarah had given her at the hospital. She'd already filled many pages with her story since The Fall, and was now to the point where she was recording thoughts and memories from the past twenty-four hours. She picked up the notebook, opened it to the place where she'd previously left off, and started writing. She wrote about the previous night, where she'd gathered around the fire with her friends and the campground survivors. She wrote about how she had been contemplating staying here when the rest of the group left to head to Washington later in the morning. For many reasons, she'd considered it, assuming that Charlie and the others would allow her to stay. Not only did she see the place as somewhere to survive away from danger, but she also found herself falling more and more for Will. She couldn't explain why, and she couldn't show him, but it was happening. And every time he kissed Holly, she fell deeper into a confused state of despair.

As she put away her notebook, she brought her knees up to her chest and looked out onto the pond. A fish jumped up, disturbing what had been a calm blanket of water. Jessica smiled, breathing in fresh air all around her.

She allowed herself another twenty minutes of basking in nature before she stood up and began to make her way back to the cabins, all with a sigh.

Upon emerging from the shadow of the trees, she came around the backside of the furthest cabin and looked across the way to see Gabriel marching down the front steps, his bag on one shoulder, a rifle over the other. From his stern facial expression, he didn't look very happy. She shifted to a quicker pace to catch up to him.

"Hey," Jessica said. "Will back yet?"

Gabriel threw his bag into the back seat of the van and then turned back to face her.

"Where the fuck did he go?"

His tone took her aback. "Um, I don't know."

"Selfish asshole," Gabriel mumbled.

"What's your problem?" Jessica asked.

"My problem? My problem is that he keeps making all the decisions as if he's the one in charge. He's not. We make decisions together, it was decided from the get-go. He can't just run off when we're supposed to be leaving this morning. It's bullshit."

Jessica stood there, staring blankly back at Gabriel. While

she did somewhat agree with him about it not being the smartest decision for Will to have left that morning, it was much more important to her that the group not have a divide. If they were going to be together in this in order to survive, everyone needed to keep a level head.

Seeing that Jessica was speechless, Gabriel became tired of waiting for a response. He scoffed, slammed the door to the van, and moved past her, bumping shoulders on the way by as he stomped back to the cabin.

CHAPTER THIRTEEN

The sky was clear, promising a gorgeous day. As they reached the bottom of the mountain, Will reached his hand out the window to enjoy the breeze.

Before they'd gone to bed the previous night, Charlie had mentioned a camping retailer a couple of exits down from the Home Depot. Charlie felt good about the prospect of there being generators there, but when he and Thomas had gone to the store before to scope it out, they hadn't even exited off the interstate. The parking lot had been overpowered with Empties. Even though Thomas had wanted to give it a go, Charlie had refused. They'd only had one rifle and a couple of handguns with them, all of which belonged to Thomas, and Charlie had felt like they wouldn't stand a chance. Now, with more firearms, Charlie had decided he wanted to try again. Charlie had wanted to ask Thomas to come along, but he had been MIA all evening while others sat outside by the campfire. He'd even knocked on Thomas' cabin door that morning, but to no answer. Will had told Charlie that he wanted to go under the radar, as his group might have tried and stopped him from going — specifically, Gabriel. But he felt that they owed Charlie for bringing them into their camp, especially after holding him and Claire both at gunpoint. The only person who'd been awake when they left the camp was Scott. It took some convincing on Charlie's part, but he'd been able to convince Scott to come with them.

At the bottom of the mountain, Charlie followed the same path that they'd come before to head up to the campsite. He turned onto the interstate, heading East.

"How far down is it?" Will asked.

"Just a couple of exits," Charlie said.

"And exactly how many of them did you see out there?" Scott asked, thinking of the Empties.

"If I had to guess, probably thirty or so," Charlie said. "I drove by once more two days ago, and the parking lot was practically vacant. Maybe they'd all gone inside or maybe they'd left, I don't know. Wasn't going to risk it to find out."

"Well, thanks for waiting to bring me with you," Scott said, a nervous tremble in his voice.

"Hey, you didn't have to come," Charlie said.

Will said, "Don't worry, Scott. If it looks to be dangerous, we're not going in."

A couple of miles down the road, after maneuvering around vacant cars and a small horde of Empties, the large outdoor store came into view, it simply being called Outdoors Unlimited. The parking lot appeared to be calm from a distance. The only thing Will saw outside the store were some boats and some camper trailers. A camper could be something for the group to consider snagging from the place when they hit the road again, though Will wasn't sure if the amount of gas it would eat up would be worth it, especially considering how scarce they'd found fuel to be.

Charlie took the exit for Parker Avenue, turning toward Outdoors Unlimited at the end of the ramp. The store took up a large plot of land, and the only other business nearby was a gas station, which Charlie informed Will that they'd already checked for fuel. Other than that, the land was open. People either took this exit to get gas, go buy shit to camp with, or continued down Parker Avenue for apparently some time before they'd likely hit civilization again.

The front of the store came into view, and it was clear that most of the glass on the front of the building had been shattered. Shopping carts lay sprawled on the sidewalk outside the store's entrance, and many of the parking spots remained occupied by vehicles.

"There's likely to be Empties inside," Will said.

Charlie nodded in agreement.

Will said, "Kinda hard to believe there's any campers left out front. You'd think this place would have been completely raided by now."

"Not a lot of population in this area," Charlie said. "Only gets busy around here during vacation season. During school, it's dead."

"That's why me and my buddies waited to come down now," Scott said.

Now that they could see the entire scope of the store's lot, Will saw the few Empties that loitered outside. One of the weapons that they'd brought with them was a machete that belonged to Thomas. Will reached to the floorboard and grabbed the weapon.

"See if you can pull up beside that one so I can take it out with this," Will said, pointing toward one of the creatures just up ahead.

With two hands on the grip of the machete, Will leaned out the window as Charlie lined the vehicle up so they'd pull in beside the beast.

Will said, "Be sure to go in with some speed."

The creature snarled as the SUV came up beside it, and Will let out a warrior's grunt as he reared back the machete, timing his swing perfectly. He'd closed his eyes halfway through the blow, but felt the blade connect with the creature, muting its snarl. Blood shot up onto the side of the SUV. Charlie and Scott reacted from inside the SUV with victorious cries, and Will looked back to see the headless body spill over onto the ground.

"Let's get the other two so we can head inside," Will said.

They took out the next Empty almost verbatim to the way they'd destroyed the first. When Charlie went for the drive by the third creature, it moved at the last minute and got clipped by the front of the vehicle. Will still swung, nearly throwing himself out of the truck with all the momentum he'd carried through the swing. Once Charlie had confirmed Will wasn't going to fall, he stopped the vehicle.

"Here," Charlie said, asking Will for the machete. Will handed him the weapon and Charlie stepped outside.

The creature lay on the ground about fifteen yards back from the vehicle. Its right leg was twisted around, having been caught by the front end of the SUV. It still tried to stand, reaching its decrepit arm out toward Charlie. Charlie kicked the thing's hanging limb out of the way, pulled back, and swung the blade down across the beast's throat. Its arm dropped as blood sprayed up, and then settled to a pour onto the concrete. Charlie turned and headed back to the vehicle.

"Nice swing," Will said as Charlie reloaded into the driver's seat.

Smiling, Charlie said, "Golf team in high school."

"You don't look like a golfer," Scott said.

"Yeah, neither did Tiger," Charlie said.

Will laughed. "Come on, let's go see if we can find us a generator."

Charlie drove to the front of the store, and with the windows down, they could hear the snarls from inside.

"Pull to the side," Will said.

Veering away from the shattered front of the store, Charlie pulled the vehicle around the side of the building, parking in a vacant handicap spot. Will pulled the rifle from the floorboard, confirming it was loaded. He tossed extra rounds into his coat pocket.

"Did you guys hear that?" Scott asked from the back seat, a tremble in his voice.

"Yeah," Will said, confirming the ammunition was secure in his pocket. "Sounds like a lot of 'em."

"Why don't we wait until we can bring the rest of the group down here?" Scott asked.

Will said, "Because my group is going to want to leave when I get back."

Charlie looked back to Scott and said, "We won't go in if it looks too dangerous, alright? But let's at least go up front and have a peek inside. You got that shotgun loaded?"

Scott bowed his head, looking down at the gun in his hands. "Yeah," he mumbled.

"Good," Will said. "Let's go."

Will led the three men toward the front door. He ducked under the shattered windows that lined the front. As they'd heard from the vehicle, there were many snarls coming from inside the building. They were so jumbled together, like a wall of sound, that it was hard to tell just how many Empties could be lurking in the store.

Will stopped beside the front door, staying in a squat with his back against the building. He poked his head around the corner and looked inside. Just at the front of the store, around the cash registers, he saw four beasts lumbering around. He also noticed the chewed-up remains of two bodies lying just inside the doors. He jerked his head away, the smell in the air matching what he'd just seen. He looked over to Charlie and reported to them the situation inside.

"It's a big store," Scott said. "No telling how many more of them could be in there."

Will looked over to Charlie and said, "So, what do you think?"

Charlie drew in a deep breath and bit his lip. He reached under his shirt, grabbing something at the end of a necklace and closing his eyes for a moment. He threw the rifle off of his shoulder and set it on the ground, and then he reached into his pocket and came out holding the keys to the SUV. He offered them to Will.

"Be ready to start that car."

Will narrowed his eyes and shook his head. "What are you doing? You're not going in there alone."

Charlie stood and drew his sidearm, a .45. It shook in his hands as he stepped toward the front door. Will reached out and grabbed Charlie's pant leg.

"Charlie, wait. Let's come up with a plan."

"Just cover me," Charlie said, not even looking down.

He ran inside, and the first gunshot went off.

CHAPTER FOURTEEN

As it turned out, the four creatures at the front of the store stood as just an appetizer.

Will hurried to his feet and turned in front of the entrance to the store. The first gunshot he'd heard had apparently been Charlie taking out one of the creatures, as now only three stood before him. He noticed blood pooling on the floor from the other side of a checkout lane. When he looked past the front of the store, he saw more undead beings lumbering through the aisles. Some of them headed toward the front of the store while others headed for the back left corner of the retail outlet.

"Scott, I need your help," Will said.

When he looked down to Scott, the fresh college graduate sat motionless with his back against the front of the building. Motionless except for the slight quake in his arms and his face.

"Scott!" Will yelled, and Scott still didn't move. Will fired his gun at one of the creatures, then kicked Scott.

"If you wanna make it out of here alive," Will said, his gun aimed inside the store and his eyes narrowed down at Scott, "I suggest you get to your fucking feet, pump that shotgun, and help me out!"

Somehow, Scott managed himself to his feet, even on his shaky legs. He staggered to the entrance of the store, and his eyes widened as he saw the group of Empties coming for them.

"Fuck, man. Fuck," Scott said.

Will set the rifle on his shoulder and said, "Just remember to breathe, and try to aim for their heads. But you've got enough kick in that thing where, even if you just hit 'em in the body, it'll knock 'em down. Probably even break off a limb, depending on your aim. If you're not gonna go for their heads, try to take out their legs." He handed Scott the keys to the SUV. "Stay behind me, and be ready to get back to the SUV and start it."

Will stepped into the entranceway of the store, being sure not to trip on the bodies on the ground. Drawing in a deep breath, Will took aim at a creature coming down a checkout lane. Its mouth opened wide as it screamed at him. He waited for the thing to get close enough where he knew he wouldn't miss, and then he squeezed the trigger and watched as half the creature's face flew off, and the body fell to the floor.

Will turned his attention to the next Empty, which knocked down a free-standing display before coming into full view. He shot again, hitting this one in the shoulder. The creature staggered back, but stayed on its feet. Will breathed and then shot again, this time catching the beast beside its eye.

The time Will lost by hitting the creature in the shoulder with his first shot allowed for the other Empties to move in closer. He moved down to his left in the wide open space that stood between the front of the store and the checkout lanes. Seven more Empties remained by Will's quick count, and they were all approaching the checkout lanes, getting closer with every passing second. Not helping the situation, Scott had yet to take a shot.

Will shouted, "Scott, I need you! Now!"

Moving to his left, Will put the rifle to his shoulder again and aimed at another beast. He was about to pull the trigger when something slammed against a wall and screamed behind him. Will looked back, staring through the small window of a door at the face of an Empty. It appeared to have once been a woman, an employee of the store, and was trapped inside a tiny administrative office.

"Shit," he mumbled, breathing heavy.

Will turned around again, and his eyes went wide as an Empty lunged at him. He instinctively held up his rifle and the thing bit into it, just missing his hand. Will pushed the beast away, but he lost his grip on his firearm. The Empty stood a few yards in front of him, the rifle having fallen down to its feet. The Empty lunged at Will again, but before its slimy hands reached him, its head vanished, and blood splattered all over Will's face for the umpteenth time in the past two weeks. His ears rang from the blast, and he glanced over to see Scott with the smoking barrel of his shotgun still pointed toward where the Empty had once stood. The boom of the shotgun banging around in his head, Will gained his composure enough to bend over and retrieve his own rifle. As he locked it back to his shoulder, Scott turned and screamed as he fired another slug, catching an Empty in the shoulder and severing its arm clean from its socket. He seemed to be having fun now, as he smiled and laughed.

Another beast came down checkout lane number eight, and Will used a single shot to send the thing to the ground. After he finished reloading the rifle, he looked up to see that none of the Empties were left. Scott had gone on a rampage to finish them off, and he now stood halfway down one of the checkout lanes, breathing heavily, with the shotgun down at his side.

"Go!"

The voice came from the rear of the store. Will looked up, but was at a weird angle where he couldn't see past a large wall.

Scott moved to the front of the lane he was standing in, and stared down to the other end of the store. His eyes opened wide.

"What?" Will asked, moving to the entrance of the store, still unable to see.

Without a word, Scott hurried out the door, fishing the keys to the SUV out of his pocket.

Will heard footsteps approaching fast, and walked down one of the aisles to see for himself who or what was coming. He stood in the open space between the checkout lanes and the individual aisles.

"Oh, shit."

Charlie ran, dragging a generator on wheels behind him. Just beyond him was possibly the largest horde of Empties Will had seen yet. It had to be made up of twenty or thirty of the creatures.

Waving his arms, Charlie yelled, "Go! Get to the truck!"

Will turned, stumbling over the leg of a wire display and almost falling to the ground. He managed to stay on his feet and run for the door.

Just as he exited the store, the SUV came to a halt in front of the building, the tires screeching and the back end fishtailing.

Will ran around to the backside of the vehicle, opening the rear cargo door.

"Once we've got this generator loaded, just be ready to get us the fuck out of here," Will said, shouting up to Scott in the driver's seat.

"Here he comes," Scott said, staring out the passenger side window.

Charlie emerged from the front of the store, and Will waved him to the rear of the truck. Will looked in the cargo area and realized, with all the confusion, he'd forgotten to lower the back seats so that the generator would fit.

"Shit."

He reached inside, looking for the button to get the seats down. Charlie arrived, panting and sweating.

"We've gotta get this inside, now!" Charlie said.

"I can't get the seats down."

Charlie opened the rear passenger side door and initiated the button that laid the seats down. Snarling came from the front of the store, and the head of the first Empty appeared. Charlie hurried around to the back and squatted down to lift the generator. Will lifted the other side, and they loaded it into the truck.

Will shut the cargo door, and followed Charlie around to the side of the truck. Charlie jumped into the back seat, but three Empties were too close. Will pulled the rifle up to his shoulder, and unloaded into the creatures. It took four shots, but he took them all down, just before a larger group poured out of the front door.

"Get your ass in here!" Scott yelled.

Will loaded into the passenger seat, and Scott raced away from the store before Will could even shut his door.

CHAPTER FIFTEEN

"But I don't wanna leave," Dylan said. He was still sitting in the bed, the covers pulled up to his waist.

"I'm sorry," Gabriel said. "This isn't our home. We have to go." He left the room and headed into the kitchen, seeing what he could find to throw in his bag.

"I wanna stay here," Dylan said. He stood in the doorway now, wearing the same shirt and pants he'd been wearing the previous day. "Mr. Larry was gonna teach me how to fish today."

"Mr. Larry isn't your dad," Gabriel said. "Your dad is in—"

"Yeah, and neither are you!" Dylan spat back.

"Yes," Gabriel said, breathing deep and trying to keep himself from snapping at the boy. "But I'm responsible for you, and I'm going to get you home."

"Why? Just because you found me in that plane?" Dylan yelled.

"Dylan…"

"I wish I'd just died on that plane!" Dylan slammed the door to the bedroom.

Gabriel let out a deep sigh, leaning over the kitchen counter. He looked up at the wooden cabinet, and punched it as hard as he could, driving his fist straight through the thin, Chinese-made cabinetry. Glasses on the other side shattered. He pulled out his hand, revealing bloody knuckles. He picked a rag up off the counter, and looked over toward the door to see Holly standing inside the cabin. Her arms crossed, she scowled at him.

"How long've you been standing there?" Gabriel asked.

"Long enough to hear that poor kid wish that he were dead," Holly said. "What the hell are you doing, Gabriel?"

"What the hell am I doing?" Gabriel pulled the rag away from his hand, which had once been white, but now soaked with blood. "You're gonna pin this on me? I wouldn't even be in the mood I'm in if it weren't for that shithead running out of here, making his own decisions without us," he said, speaking of Will. "I mean, where the hell did he even go?"

Holly shook her head and started toward Dylan's room.

"What?" Gabriel said. "Tell me, where did he go?"

Holly turned around and said, "Look around you. Stop being so Goddam selfish and try thinking about other people for a change." She turned back and knocked on Dylan's door, saying his name. The door opened and she went inside.

Before the door closed again, Gabriel met eyes with Dylan. The boy's face was flushed from crying.

Holly shut the door, and Gabriel leaned over the counter. He rubbed his forehead with his uninjured hand and sighed.

"Son of a bitch," he mumbled.

The sound of tires kicking up rocks sounded outside and Gabriel turned toward the front of the cabin. He walked over to the door and opened it. Brake lights shined on a SUV, and the engine shut off. Others emerged from the cabins across the courtyard as Will stepped out of the vehicle. He looked as if he'd been dropped in the middle of a war, his front side drenched in blood. Behind Gabriel, the door to Dylan's room opened and he emerged with Holly, both of them hurrying over to the door. Gabriel stepped all the way out onto the front porch, allowing room for Holly and Dylan to come through the door. Holly used her hand as a visor and gasped. She darted down the porch steps and raced over to Will. She hugged him, he picking her up into his arms. Gabriel looked off to his right and saw Jessica staring down at Will and Holly. She looked over, her eyes meeting Gabriel's, and then she turned around and went back inside.

Dylan exited the cabin and started for the steps. Gabriel grabbed the boy by the shoulder, and Dylan looked up.

"I'm sorry," Gabriel said.

Dylan shrugged Gabriel's hand off and continued for the stairs, mumbling, "Whatever."

Though the day had brought with it a cool Autumn chill, Gabriel stood sweating. His nerves crawled on his arms like hundreds of spiders, and his head began to throb. It felt like someone pressing the heels of their palms against both of his temples. He'd been so distracted that he'd forgotten about his injured hand. He looked down and saw that he'd dropped the rag onto the porch, and blood seeped from his hand onto the wooden slats. He went back inside the cabin, grabbed another rag, applied pressure to his hand, and then made his way across the front porch.

Charlie and Scott worked to unload the generator out of the back of the SUV. Like Will, both of the men looked like they'd been through hell. They set the generator down onto the ground, and then Charlie walked over to Will and extended his hand.

"Brother, thanks again for helping us out."

Will laughed. "You're the crazy son of a bitch that ran into that store."

Charlie shrugged. "Gotta do what we gotta do, man."

"I guess," Will said, still smiling.

Charlie turned around to Scott and said, "Let's roll this thing over by our cabins for now. We'll talk to everyone else in a little bit and see where the best place to put this will be."

Gabriel approached Will, who turned and smiled at him, as if everything were cool.

"Morning, man," Will said. "What's up?"

Not slowing his gait, Gabriel sprung his arms and shoved Will in his shoulders, sending him down into the dirt.

"What're you doing?" Holly said. She turned to Dylan and said, "Go inside."

"No, I—"

"Now," Holly said, making sure her tone conveyed to the boy that she wasn't offering him a choice. Dylan pushed past Gabriel and slowly made his way up to the cabin, taking his time and looking back.

Will's expression had turned from a smile to a look of disgust as he jumped back to his feet.

"What the fuck?" Will said.

"You're asking me 'what the fuck'?" Gabriel said. "You've got to be kidding me. Where the hell've you been all morning?"

"Well, considering how these people were nice enough to bring us into their community here and offer us food, shelter, a place where we could all be fucking normal for a change, I thought I'd return the favor and go help them pick up a generator."

Gabriel glanced over to see that Charlie and Scott had stopped, standing only about fifteen yards away. They watched the scene unfold. Gabriel refocused his attention to Will, taking a step toward him to cut their distance in half, now standing where their chests almost bumped.

"You don't think saving his life at that store yesterday was enough?" Gabriel said, keeping his attention on Will but pointing his finger toward Charlie.

"You blind, Gabriel? They might've saved *our* lives. Four whole cans of fuel? You think they really have to give us all that?"

Gabriel scoffed. "Whatever. Just get your shit together so that we can get the hell outta here." He turned around and started back toward the cabin, looking around the campground to see that everyone was outside now, either standing in the courtyard or watching from the front porches of their respective cabins. Including Jessica, who leaned on the bannister of the front porch, shaking her head as she and Gabriel made eye contact. He looked away and continued his march back toward his cabin to grab the last of his things.

"I'm not leaving."

Gabriel stopped and turned around again, watching everyone's eyes settle on him as he did. Will stood with his arms crossed, as if he were staking his claim in the land.

"I'm staying here," Will said. "I'm tired of running. Tired of chasing some sort of false hope." He put his arm around Holly, who looked shocked, as if this were news to her, as well. He held her for a moment before letting go and stepping toward Gabriel. "Charlie offered for us to stay. All of us."

Gabriel let the words sit in the air for a moment, the anger crawling all over his arms again. Even though the day was cool, it felt as if the sun was baking him. But that was just his internal heat rising.

He had no response for Will. He simply turned, kicking the gravel as he swung around, and stormed back to his cabin.

***

Gabriel made one last pass through the cabin, making sure he'd gathered all his things. He went into Dylan's room and began transferring the boy's few possessions from the bed to a bag. The bathroom door opened and Dylan came into the room.

"What are you doing?" Dylan asked.

"We're leaving," Gabriel said.

"I'm not going," Dylan said.

Gabriel turned around to face the boy. He said, "Yes, you are. We're not stopping anymore, and we're gonna get to Virginia and find your parents."

"But I heard Will say he isn't going. Is Mary Beth?"

Gabriel ignored the question and turned back to the bed, and zipped up Dylan's bag. He picked it up and walked it over to him.

"Just take this and load it into the van."

"You didn't answer my question," Dylan said. "I'm not going without her."

The front door of the cabin opened and Jessica emerged. Dylan ran over to her.

"Tell Gabriel that I don't have to go," Dylan said. "Please." He had tears in his eyes now, and Gabriel could feel a new brand of guilt ride up into his gut. This wasn't the first time he'd had trouble with Dylan over his decisions, and he knew, just like before, that the kid would get over it.

"You can't make him go with us if he doesn't want to go, Gabriel," Jessica said.

Gabriel narrowed his eyes. "Us?"

Jessica said, "I'm going with you. There's nothing for me here, and I want to see what we can find in D.C. To see if I can help you find your family. But you can't make Dylan go. Let him stay here. It's safe here. Let Will and Holly look after him. Let him stay with his friends and try to somewhat live a normal life."

Gabriel couldn't look at Dylan without feeling remorseful. The responsibility for the child had almost literally fallen into his lap, and he'd grown so close to Dylan. The truth was, *he* wasn't ready to let Dylan go. More than once, the thought had crossed Gabriel's mind that he would get to Alexandria and never find Dylan's parents. And with a gun to his head, Gabriel would have to have told the truth and say that he *hoped* they wouldn't find them. Even though it had only been a couple of weeks, he'd taken Dylan in like his own child. Letting him go would just leave another hole in Gabriel's heart.

But as he looked into the boy's eyes, he knew what the right decision was.

***

Most everyone at the camp gathered around to see Gabriel and Jessica off. Gabriel had calmed down, though he hadn't changed his mind about leaving. He had no other option. The simple thought that he'd already wasted too much time and had possibly missed the opportunity to save his own family weighed heavily on him.

Gabriel and Jessica each walked down the line of people, shaking the hands of the survivors from the campground first. All of them were present except for Thomas, who'd remained strangely absent. Jessica thanked each one of them, and Gabriel followed, simply acknowledging each of the individuals without repeating the same pleasantries as Jessica. Holly and Will stood near the end of the line. Once Jessica was done hugging each of them, Gabriel stepped up. Though he and Holly had had it out earlier, she still allowed him to give her a hug, as well as a kiss on the cheek. He then moved in front of Will, and the two men just looked at each other. Gabriel could feel everyone's eyes on them, as if they were waiting for a fight to break out. He then looked down and saw that Will had his hand extended out. Gabriel waited a moment, then accepted the handshake.

"You sure you wanna do this?" Will asked.

Gabriel responded, "Are you?"

Will nodded.

And that was the extent of their conversation.

Gabriel now drew in a deep breath as he arrived at the three children. He shook Reece's hand, then looked down to Dylan and Mary Beth. She had her arm around Dylan as he cried. Gabriel leaned down to eye-level with them.

He said to Mary Beth, "You take care of him now, you hear?"

She smiled and nodded, saying, "Yes, sir."

And when his eyes met Gabriel's, Dylan let go of Mary Beth and embraced Gabriel, letting out all of his emotion. The small hands gripped the back of Gabriel's shirt tightly.

"Don't go," Dylan pleaded.

"I've got to," Gabriel said. "You know that. I've got to find my wife and my little girl. Once I find them, perhaps I will bring them back here if there's no refuge in Washington."

Dylan didn't respond. He just held Gabriel and cried. Gabriel's gaze shifted to the other, particularly to Will and Holly. He could see in both their faces that they both hated his decision to leave, but also that they understood it. Gabriel just hoped that splitting from the group would turn out better than it had the last time he'd tried to go out on his own.

Gabriel pulled away from Dylan, his hands gripping the boy's shoulders tight. He jostled Dylan's hair, choking back his own tears. He wanted to stay strong for the kid, but it was growing more difficult with every passing moment.

A door to one of the cabins slamming drew everyone's attention. Leaving one hand on Dylan's shoulder, Gabriel used his other hand as a visor to block out the sun and look toward the commotion. Thomas had emerged from his cabin, lugging a suitcase-on-wheels behind him and carrying his rifle over his shoulder. The silence among the other survivors said it all.

Claire split from the others, walking toward her brother, and said, "What are you doing?"

"I'm leaving," Thomas said, marching toward the van.

"What?" Claire said. She moved from beside him to in front of him, halting in his path so that he would come to a top. "What do you mean you're leaving?"

"I'm going with them to Virginia," Thomas said. "I'm tired of sitting around here doing nothing. Someone in Washington has to know something about what's going on or how to stop this demonic plague." He looked over to Will. "Claire told me about what you know. About what happened to you. That information is far too important not to try and get it to Washington."

Will looked on, his arm wrapped around Holly.

Thomas went to throw his bag into the open sliding door of the van, but Claire stopped him. He turned back to her, eyes almost crossed in frustration.

"Claire, let go. You're not stopping me from leaving."

Claire said, "No, I'm not. But I'm not letting you leave without me. And if I'm leaving, I'm not leaving my car here."

**

Gabriel and Jessica transferred their things to Claire's SUV, while Claire had retreated to her cabin to gather her things. Once she came back outside, ready to load her things and leave, Gabriel left Will with some of the ammunition he'd gathered, now that Thomas had decided to come, bringing with him a small arsenal.

"Thanks," Will said.

Gabriel nodded and turned around to load into the cockpit of the SUV. He'd be taking the first driving shift.

Will said, "Hey."

Gabriel looked back.

"Good luck finding Katie and Sarah."

With a nod, his lips pursed, Gabriel said, "Thanks, brother."

He shut the door and clicked on his seatbelt. When he looked back out, Dylan stood staring, his eyes mostly dry now. Gabriel waved and gave the boy a thumbs-up, and Dylan waved back.

Before he had any second thoughts about leaving, Gabriel looked away, drawing his attention to the rearview mirror as he backed up. Dirt appeared in the reflection, the tires sending it into the clean, mountain air.

He started down the dirt path of the mountain, and he didn't look back until they turned around a corner, and he glanced into the rearview mirror again.

All he saw were trees and dust.

CHAPTER SIXTEEN

They watched as the headlights to Claire's SUV disappeared around the corner through the trees. Dylan's tears flowed freely now, and the boy allowed all his emotion to drain out of him. Holly left Will's side and hugged Dylan, patting him on the back and assuring him that everything would be fine.

At once, a whole new thought came to Will. Essentially, he'd instantly become a father. Dylan and Mary Beth were his and Holly's responsibility now. Sure, the others at the campground would help out, but they were by no means required to. Will and Holly had inherited the liability of the two children the moment that he'd informed Gabriel he was staying at the cabins. Still trying to come to grips with losing his own parents, he wasn't sure how he would handle this new responsibility. Will did want kids, and perhaps even with Holly, but under a different circumstance than this.

Holly looked up to Will and said, "I'm gonna take him to his cabin and start getting his stuff moved over to ours. Is that okay?"

"Yeah, that's fine." Will looked down, reminding himself of the clothes he was in, still disgusting from the run-in with all the beasts at the camping store. "I'm gonna go clean up and lie down for a while."

As Holly headed away with Dylan, Mary Beth followed. Will started for his cabin, but was stopped by Charlie.

"You okay?" Charlie asked.

"Yeah," Will mumbled. "I'm all good. Just tired."

"Me, too. Let's both get some rest and catch up in a little while, alright?"

"Sounds like a plan," Will said.

***

Dylan's things had already been packed up, as Gabriel had assumed the boy would be leaving with him. This made it fairly simple for Holly to take Dylan back to his cabin to grab his things. Mary Beth had gone to hang out with Reece for a little while, leaving Holly and Dylan alone. While Reece slept each night in the same cabin as Scott, he'd often spend a large part of his day in one of the unoccupied cabins, where they kept some of the board and card games. This particular cabin had become simply known as 'the game room'.

Holly looked around in the cabinets, seeing if there was anything worth taking. It appeared to have already been cleared out. She saw the cabinet with the hole in it, and Gabriel's blood still pooled on the counter below it.

"Gabriel took most of that stuff with him," Dylan said, standing in the middle of the living room with his bag over his shoulder.

Holly shut the cabinet. They had plenty of food among the other cabins, so it wasn't a big deal. It had started to look as if the only things they'd be able to salvage out of the cabin, aside from the living space itself if they ended up needing it, were blankets, pillows, and some leftover firewood.

"I'm sure he'll need it," Holly said.

The pain remained in the boy's eyes. Holly sighed and walked to the middle of the room, where Dylan stood. She took his hand and led him over to the sofa. Sitting down, she patted the spot next to her and offered him a seat, which he accepted.

Dylan said, "Why did he have to leave? Why couldn't he have

just stayed here with us?"

"You know the answer to that, sweetie," Holly said. "Gabriel has people he loves back home. He wants to get back to them." Holly reassured him of this even though she questioned what Gabriel might or might not find when, and *if*, he made it back home.

"We should be his family. After everything we've been through together." Dylan spoke with a type of aggression that Holly hadn't heard from him before.

"It's easy to say that when you consider even just the last few days we've had," Holly said. "And I know it feels like we've been together for a long time, but it hasn't been that long. Gabriel has a daughter around your age, and he's been with his wife much longer than that. One day, when you're older and you're married, you'll have a better understanding of what kind of burden that kind of responsibility bears on you."

"I'm never getting married," Dylan said.

Holly laughed. "I don't think you'll have to worry about that anytime soon." She stood up and grabbed Dylan's bag for him. "Now, come on, let's get you over to Reece's so you can play for a while."

***

The season's first chilled night had come, as lights flashed all around. Large speakers amplified the voices of carnies trying to lure children over, all to steal their parents' hard-earned money by distracting the kids with large plush dolls that could be bought at the store for half the price it would cost to obtain enough tickets to possibly win one. Luckily for Walt Kessler, his eleven-year-old son, Will, was much more interested in experiences and food than prizes, wanting to do nothing but ride the rides and stuff his face with sugary funnel cakes and nachos covered in anything and everything to clog arteries.

Will walked beside his father, eating his second slice of pizza of the evening. Two slices was nothing to Will normally, but after the two hot dogs, a cup of ice cream, funnel cake, and sharing nachos with his father, he was at the point of bursting. Even still, he wanted to ride anything that would twist him sideways or turn him upside down. His stomach ached, but he wouldn't let that ruin the rest of his night at the state fair with his father, an annual tradition they'd stayed true to for as long as Will had been tall enough to meet the height requirements of most of the rides.

"What you wanna do next?"

Will looked up to see his father smiling down at him. His eyes then shifted forward, gazing upon 'Starship 5000', one of those spaceship rides where you're inside a round, UFO type structure, and it spins fast enough to make you move up and down on the wall you're strapped to, almost defying gravity. Will remembered one of his friends telling him that, if you spit while inside there, your flem would fly around the ship at the speed of a NASCAR, but he'd never had the guts to try it.

"That!" Will said, pointing to it. "I wanna ride 'Starship 5000'."

Walt Kessler laughed. "Son, if you ride that thing, you're gonna make a lot of people inside very angry when you plaster the walls with pizza and ice cream."

"Cool!" Will said.

Walt scanned the lay of the land, and he pointed to their left.

"How about you go inside that? Do something a little more laid-back."

Will looked over to see his father pointing at a fun house. It was one of those really cheesy ones with a bunch of clowns painted on the side, working to try and scare people who are frightened by weird guys in colorful make-up and green wigs. Will wasn't one of those people.

"Dad, come on, that's lame."

He closed his eyes as his father rustled his hair. His dad nodded toward the fun house, and urged his son to follow him.

"Come on," Walt said.

Will let out a long sigh and followed his father, chewing his way down to the crust of his pizza — his favorite part, especially when it had a touch of cinnamon added to it like this slice did. He wiped his hands and then disposed of the napkin in a trash can.

Leaning down and handing Will three tickets, Walt patted his son on the back and said, "I'll be out here, alright?"

"You're really gonna make me go in there?" Will asked.

"Look, there's not even a line," his father said. "Come on, you might have fun. Who knows?"

Of course there's not a line, Will thought. 'Cause it's lame. He let out a deep breath and said, "Fine."

His father smiled. "I'll be right here." He urged Will toward the funhouse, then leaned back against a guard rail, withdrawing a pack of cigarettes from his pocket.

Will was the fifth kid in line for 'Clown Town', standing behind kids who were all younger than he was. He glanced back to his father, who blew a cloud of smoke in the air, smiling at his son and waving.

When he reached the front of the line, the carney said, "Three tickets, please," which Will reluctantly handed over to the guy with slicked-back hair, who smelled like a combination of every fried food stand that he'd passed, and the disgusting aftershave that Principal Crossley always wore.

"Go on in," the carney said.

It was just as lame as Will had known it would be. He had to enter the funhouse on a bridge that quaked in a way that tried to make you think you wouldn't make it across. In truth, his friend Hunter's two-legged dog could have made it across. Once on the other side, repeated laughter came from speakers which sounded like they were part of the first stereo system ever made. He could hear every pop and click from the tired audio. Will wanted to get out of the funhouse as fast as possible and go ride something fun. That spaceship, the Tilt-A-Whirl... something, anything, else.

Moments after a cardboard clown jumped out at him, the power inside of the funhouse faltered, and everything went black. Will stood still, waiting for power to be restored. At first, he thought it was part of the experience, but then he noticed through a window in the next room that it was dark outside. He held onto the wall and moved to the next area, looking out the window. Outside, it was pitch black. Stranger, none of the young brats in front of him were screaming. It was quiet all around him.

"Hello?" Will called out.

No answer.

He used the walls to guide himself out, the lack of power leaving the chance of some prop jumping out at him as nonexistent. Somehow, he made it to the exit of the funhouse without falling down.

When he walked outside, he stopped dead in his path.

Not only was his father gone, but the entire park was vacant.

Will stood, stunned, and said, "Dad?"

No answer.

"Dad!"

His voice echoed off the steel of the dead rides.

Off in the distance, he heard a laugh.

Will followed the sound, hearing the sound of a man laughing every ten seconds or so.

He stopped when he came to a gate. A large sign above it read: Emergency Exit. A banner covered the opposite side of the rod-iron fence, making it impossible to see the other side.

The lock on the gate popped, and it started to swing open, the creak echoing into Will's ears. He stepped toward the fence with caution, curious as to what lay on the other side. The laugh faded, and now he heard something else.

Growls.

Snarling.

Will's eyes widened, and he tripped over the untied shoelaces of his Chucks.

A horde of undead monsters lumbered toward him. Their faces were pale, their hair matted and dry. They looked like creatures he'd fought in video games and seen in movies.

He gasped for air as he stumbled back to his feet, and started to run the other way without looking. But he hit something, knocking him back down onto the concrete.

And when he looked up, he saw a familiar face.

"Dad?"

But it wasn't his dad at all. Not anymore. Walt Kessler had turned into one of the monsters. Using his father's eyes, the thing looked down at Will, moving its tongue over its dry lips and snarling. Will used his hands to crawl backward, turning around to see the hundreds of others approaching closer. He was trapped.

The laugh returned, and Will cocked his head. It sounded so familiar. Not to pre-teen Will Kessler, but to adult Will Kessler.

It was unmistakable.

The sky opened, revealing the face of David Ellis. Will's eyes widened, and the sky laughed again just as his father lunged toward his face.

***

Will woke up screaming. It echoed through the entire cabin. He rolled onto his side from his back to confirm he was no longer dreaming. It had felt so real.

The door swung open and Holly appeared in the doorway. She darted to the side of the bed.

Will kicked off the sheets, which had become damp, the intensity of the dream lunging him into a cold sweat. He sat up, pushing himself back against the headboard, and rubbed his forehead.

"I'm fine," he said. "Just another bad dream."

Holly grabbed his hand, but he jerked it away. She cocked her head and narrowed her eyes in surprise and frustration.

"I'm sorry. I'm just not in the mood to be touched right now."

"I understand," Holly said.

Will kicked the covers the rest of the way off of him, and massaged his temples. His head had begun to ache.

"What was it about?" Holly asked. "David? Your parents?"

Will thought back to his vivid memory of that trip to the state fair with his father. They'd gone every year until he'd turned sixteen and been old enough to drive there with his buddies. The time he'd dreamed about was one of the most vivid memories because, unlike in the dream, he had gone on the 'Starship 5000' and he'd gotten very ill, vomiting during the ride. Just before jumping on that ride, Will's father had joked with him about going into 'Clown Town' instead, knowing his son had no interest in that.

"Yeah," Will mumbled.

"Is there anything I can do for you?"

Will rubbed his eyes, then looked to her and said, "I just need some time to wake up. Can you give me a few minutes? Maybe see if you can find any aspirin?"

"Of course," Holly said. "I'll see what I can find and I'll meet you out in the living room."

"Thanks," Will said, and he leaned in, then kissed her.

Holly smiled. "I'm really glad we decided to stay here."

"Me, too," Will said, running his hand through her dark blonde hair. "Me, too."

CHAPTER SEVENTEEN

When he had finished showering, Will dressed himself in something warm and headed out into the living room. As he entered, the heat from the fireplace hit him, having a calming effect. Holly had put a blanket down on the floor in front of the fireplace and was lying on her side. Even with all they'd been through, her face still showed the same beauty Will had noticed when he first saw her at the end of the loading dock at Ellis Metals, it now reflecting in the light of the flames. She smiled as he entered the room.

"Charlie came by," Holly said. "He said he had something important to talk to you about. He wanted to try and discuss it with you before dinner."

"When's that?"

"I think in about an hour or so."

Will asked, "Where are the kids?"

"Playing board games with Reece," Holly said.

Will approached Holly, kneeling down beside her. Even in the oversized clothes she wore now to stay warm, her curves were obvious underneath. He joined her on the blanket, facing his back to the fire and wrapping his arm around her. He ran his hand through her hair, and kissed her on the lips.

He smiled and said, "That gives us plenty of time."

***

Charlie opened the door before Will even had the chance to knock. He smiled and moved aside, allowing Will to enter his cabin.

"You look a lot better," Charlie said.

"Likewise," Will said, noticing Charlie had cleaned himself up, as well, since their expedition earlier. "How's Scott?"

"Pretty sure he's still asleep at his place," Charlie said. He looked outside, then said, "Holly not with you?"

Will shook his head. "She went to check on the kids. She need to be here?"

The sound of the toilet flushing came from the bathroom, and its door opened. Larry, one half of the older couple at the campground, came walking into the main room, adjusting the belt on his pants.

"No," Charlie said. "You can fill her in later."

"Alright," Will said.

Will sat down on the loveseat, and Charlie offered him a glass of water.

"Thanks," Will said, accepting the glass.

Larry sat in the recliner across the room, groaning as his joints popped from the change in his body's form.

"So," Will said, "what's up?"

Charlie took a sip of his water, leaving it just under a quarter full. "I think we may know somewhere where we might be able to get some answers."

"About?" Will inquired.

Charlie looked to the place on Will's sleeved arm, where his wounds were. "About what happened to you. About what's happening to everyone."

Will glanced back and forth between the two men, focusing on what they'd say next.

"My late brother, God bless his soul," Larry said, "had a good friend over in Raleigh. A preacher. He was heavily involved with a large Catholic mega-church in Durham. I've seen the place with my own eyes. It's huge."

"So, you think your brother's friend might be there and can help us?" Will said.

Larry shook his head. "Part of the church is an enormous library. One time, I was at a family get-together and Father Ted, my brother's friend, was there. I remember him talking about how all kinds of old books were there at this church library. He talked of it like it was almost a relic, or a sanctuary for aspiring priests. Well, for all Catholics who give a darn about their faith, anyway."

"The drive is only a couple of hours from here," Charlie said.

"So, you're thinking we should go there and scour through thousands of books, trying to find an answer to all this?" Will said.

"It wouldn't hurt anything," Charlie said. "We'll get up and go early in the morning, and we'll be back before dark."

"We could spend hours looking through books there. Especially if it's as big as you're saying," Will said, looking to Larry. "That's all assuming that we can even get there. I stayed with you guys because I'm tired of being out there. I'm tired of running."

"This isn't running away," Charlie said. "This is running right at our problems. This is looking for answers. And what if, by chance, we just so happen to come across something? We might be able to save a lot of people."

"Look," Will said. "I've been through a lot over the last few days. I'm mentally drained, and my body is tired."

"At least think about it," Charlie said. "Will you do that?"

His elbows on his knees, Will looked down into his worn palms. He closed his eyes, knowing he should just say no. His hands went to the bite wounds on his arm again, reminding him of the hell outside. Rubbing them, he thought about what Thomas had said — how the information they had could be crucial to helping find a solution to this mess. Drawing in a deep breath, Will looked back up to Charlie.

"I'll think about it, alright?"

***

After dinner, Will and Holly retreated back to their cabin. She started another fire while he sat on the sofa and kicked his legs up on the coffee table. It almost felt like a real home instead of some post-apocalyptic safe house.

Of course, the proposed trip to Durham didn't come up in conversation at dinner. The kids had been present, and the three men had decided to just keep it amongst themselves for the time being. That being said, Will knew he'd have to discuss it with Holly. Whether or not to go to Durham wasn't a decision he could make on his own.

"Good idea to let the kids go play at Reece's for a little while longer," Holly said.

"I agree," Will said. "I've got something we need to talk about anyway, before they come back."

"Okay," Holly said, letting the word carry itself out and show her hesitation. She finished getting the fire going and joined Will on the sofa, snuggling up next to him to steal his warmth while the orange glow began heating the air.

"Charlie wants me to go on a short trip," Will began.

"A trip? Where? For how long?" Holly asked.

Will told her about the large church and library two hours away. He explained to her how he had been hesitant upon first hearing about it, but now had had a change of heart, thinking there might actually be an answer somewhere inside that library. Some book or text that could explain what the hell had happened to him and how Samuel had drawn the demon out of him.

"When?" Holly asked.

"Not sure," Will said. "I haven't told them 'yes' or 'no' yet about even going. But I want to go. So, I'd imagine we'd drive out there on one of the next few mornings if I tell them I'm in."

"I'm fine with you going, but I'm going with you."

Will shook his head. "Holly, you need to stay here and be with the kids. If something happens to me —"

"Nothing's going to happen to you," Holly said. "The kids can stay here with Scott, Larry, and Marie."

Will scoffed and said, "That's comforting. A guy barely out of college, and grandma and grandpa."

"They'll be fine," Holly said. "We'll only be gone a day."

Will sighed and nodded. "Alright. I'll let Charlie know the two of us have agreed to go, and we can work on getting everything arranged with the kids."

"You gonna talk to him tonight?"

Will shrugged. "May as well." He looked off toward the fire, watching as the flames spilled out into the open part of the room, licking the air. He then looked back to Holly. "You sure you want to go?"

Holly smiled and leaned in to kiss Will on the cheek. "Go talk to him. I'll start gathering the kids things they'll need to stay at Larry and Marie's."

CHAPTER EIGHTEEN

As they approached the North Carolina-Virginia state line, the sun had headed to sleep, only just peeking over the horizon now. An exit for the Virginia Welcome Center lay just ahead.

"We should stop here for the night," Thomas said.

Gabriel shook his head. "We've still got some daylight left. We should keep driving."

"What if there isn't a good place to stop for another half an hour down the road?" Claire asked. "It'll be dark by then."

"She's right, Gabriel," Jessica said. "I've been through here before, and I know that there won't be a good place to stop for at least another thirty miles."

"Take the exit, Gabriel," Thomas said.

Gabriel sighed, and his hands trembled in frustration, gripping the wheel tight. At the last minute, he cut the wheel and exited the interstate.

"Thank you," Claire said as Gabriel pulled the SUV to the front of the building.

Four Empties loitered outside of the small building. Gabriel noticed that the glass door on the front of the structure was closed and unbroken.

"Looks like we'll be pretty safe if we can get inside," Gabriel said. "I was a little worried the windows would be busted out."

Thomas leaned in from the back seat and handed Gabriel a shotgun. He then looked to Claire and Jessica and said, "Stay in here. Gabriel and I can handle four of 'em on our own."

Gabriel accepted the shotgun, but shook his head. "Way too

loud. We don't know how many of those things are around here, but I can almost guarantee you that if we start firing off buckshot out there, we're sure to attract all of them." He passed the shotgun back to Thomas and said, "We've still got enough sunlight to safely see. Take this and hand me one of those hunting knives back there."

Thomas returned the shotgun to the back seat, then reached into the bag. He pulled his hand out, grasping onto the grip of a large knife. The stainless steel shimmered as he handed it up to Gabriel.

"I like big knives," Thomas said, smiling as he noticed Gabriel's reaction to holding the large blade. "So, how are we gonna do this?"

"Like this," Gabriel said, opening the door and stepping out of the SUV.

Gabriel walked over to the nearest Empty, which trudged away from a picnic table it had been standing around. He raised the knife and drove it into the side of the creature's head, sending it down to the ground. He looked to his right as he heard Thomas sound out a grunt, driving his own knife into the face of an Empty that had been standing near the entrance to the Welcome Center. The knife he held wasn't much smaller than the one he'd loaned Gabriel.

Gabriel stood near a brick-faced bathroom facility, separate from the Welcome Center's main office. The other creature closest to him stood near the entrance to the men's room, and another came limping out of the restroom itself. Gabriel rushed over to the first creature, driving the knife into its cheek before it could even reach its arms out. The thing fell before Gabriel could withdraw his knife, and the other Empty came all the way out of the men's room and lunged at him. Gabriel put his hands up, ready to defend against the creature, when a boom came from behind him, and the creature fell to the concrete, most of its blood splashing onto the wall while some made it onto Gabriel.

Gabriel wiped his face and turned around.

Claire stood ten yards away, her gun pointed toward where the beast had fallen. Beyond her, Gabriel watched as Thomas took down the last standing Empty in the area. Thomas wiped at his own face and glanced over before running toward his sister. Jessica had come out of the SUV and stood a few yards behind Claire.

"You okay?" Thomas asked.

Her hands trembling, Claire mumbled, "Yes."

Gabriel, unnerved by the bullet hissing by his head and just narrowly missing, shook it off and moved away from the brick wall. He walked over to Claire as Thomas reached out and lowered her gun, asking her to hand it over to him. She complied, and the two of them hugged. When they broke their embrace, Gabriel smiled.

He said, "Thanks."

"Y-you're welcome," Claire mumbled.

Gabriel checked inside the bathroom, then came out and looked to Thomas. "It's clear. Come on, let's see if we can get inside this place."

***

Just inside the front door of the Welcome Center, a body lay on the ground. It appeared to be that of a security guard, wearing the proper uniform, a gun lying near him. He didn't appear to have turned, what was left of his face following the apparent self-inflicted gunshot wound appearing to be that of a human, and not of one of the demon creatures.

Claire coughed and covered her nose.

"Just stay on your toes, guys," Gabriel said. He listened close, but didn't hear any creatures snarling inside the small building. It sounded as if it was clear of anything undead.

"What the fuck do you think happened to this guy?" Thomas asked.

Gabriel looked down to the man's hand, noticing the absence of a wedding ring. "Must've given up is all I can tell."

"We don't have to sleep in here with that thing, do we?" Claire asked, a tremble in her voice.

No one replied.

Gabriel went to the main desk and walked behind it. He quickly turned away from the rotting body lying beside the desk chair, but not before he could see that the person had been turned into an Empty. He looked over toward Thomas, who had opened an office door to check for any survivors or creatures.

"This room's clear," Thomas said.

"We've got another body over here," Gabriel said.

Claire gagged, then doubled-over and vomited onto the tile floor. Thomas hurried over to her, checking to make sure she was alright. Covering her nose, she waved him off as she stood up straight.

"I just need to step outside for a moment."

Thomas walked her to the door and opened it for her to step outside.

"We'll have to get these bodies out of here," Gabriel said. "And we need to see if we can find a supply closet with some cleaning supplies. Maybe also some candles or a can of air freshener so we can try to get this smell out of here."

"I'll look for that," Jessica said.

"Alright," Gabriel said. "In the meantime, Thomas and I can work on getting these two bodies out of here."

***

It had taken just over an hour, but the group had made the Welcome Center inhabitable. Jessica had broken into a closet between the outside bathrooms and found a slew of cleaning items, including surgical-type masks they'd used to cover their noses from the smell of rotted bodies. Gabriel and Thomas had thrown the bodies on the opposite side of a tree near the small recreation area outside. Then, together, the four of them had worked to scrub the remains of the two bodies off of the tile floor. The place smelled like a chemical plant, but that was a welcome alternative to it smelling like a pit of dead bodies.

As Gabriel scrubbed the last bit of matter off of the floor, he rose from his squat and rubbed the sweat from his brow, using his forearm. The four of them migrated to the center of the room, each taking off their gloves, as they'd finished their cleaning at almost the exact same time. Without speaking, they all came to the conclusion to step outside for a breath of fresh air.

Outside, Gabriel removed his mask, itching to breathe in the open air, but the wind wafted the smell of the dead bodies toward them. He covered his face again with the mask, and darted away from the wind's aim, stopping near the bathroom.

"Pretty fucked up when standing right outside of a bathroom smells better than standing in the open," Thomas said.

Gabriel chuckled. He tossed his rubber gloves, caked with death, into the nearby trashcan. Jessica, Thomas, and Claire followed suit. The night had fallen upon them, the moon in the sky only days away from being full. Not sure of how safe the area was, they couldn't stay outside for too long.

He went to the SUV, popping open the cargo area and grabbing his things. All he had to himself was a small duffle bag with a couple of sets of clothes in it, and a sleeping bag. He'd received the sleeping bag from Claire, as her and Thomas' family had been prepared to go camping while up in the mountains. He'd also taken one of the pillows from his cabin, giving himself a complete mobile bed.

Gabriel went back into the Welcome Center, dropping off his things before heading back to the SUV for essentials. Everything had to be unloaded in order to keep their food and weapon supply protected from possible looters. It was doubtful, but entirely possible, that someone could come by during the night and rob them. Between the four of them, they only needed one trip to unload all the common goods out of the SUV. To be safe, Thomas went back to the SUV and parked it out of sight, behind the Welcome Center.

After Thomas was finished, he came back inside, and Gabriel locked the door behind him. He took one last look outside, the night quiet and still. Then he turned around to join the rest of the group.

"I don't know about you all, but I'm exhausted," he said. "Let's get some rest."

CHAPTER NINETEEN

The following morning, Will and Holly woke early and began gathering things together for the day's trip. After informing Charlie the previous evening that he was down with going to check out the church and that Holly would be joining them, Will had suggested that they just go ahead and make the trip the following morning. He'd decided he'd rather get the trip out of the way, in hopes of being able to just rest afterward, as opposed to taking a few days off and then having to find the motivation to drive two hours through an impending wasteland. Even though he knew that, if they found something, there would likely be no rest for the foreseeable future.

Their bags on the bed, Will and Holly went through their mental checklist, making sure they had everything they needed. Holly checked off each gun they'd bring with them, which included two sidearms a piece, a rifle, and a shotgun, matching ammunition, two bowie knives, a machete, flashlights, extra batteries, a first aid kit they'd found in a cabinet in their kitchen, six bottles of water, a bag of almonds, and two bags of beef jerky. Charlie would make sure to fuel the truck they'd be taking, as well as grab three extra cans of gasoline.

"I think we're all set," Holly said.

"Good."

Will zipped up each bag and threw the ammunition and weapons bag over one shoulder, and the rifle over the other, leaving the emergency and food bag for Holly. They walked outside, loaded the gear into the vehicle, and then walked to

Larry and Marie's cabin.

Dylan and Mary Beth stood on the front porch, Larry towering behind them. He was around six foot three, and looked even taller wearing overalls.

Larry said, "Marie found some stuff to whip up some pancakes, including some syrup. Should be a fine breakfast for the kids. No one makes pancakes like Marie."

"Great," Will said, smiling. He walked up the steps and extended his hand to Larry. "Thanks for agreeing to take care of them."

"No problem," Larry said. "The Lord never did bless us with no grand babies, so we will enjoy this, even if it's just for the day. Might take Dylan here down to go fishin'." Larry rummaged the boy's hair as he said this, and Dylan only looked slightly annoyed.

"I wanna go fishing," Mary Beth said.

Larry laughed. "You can go, too, young lady."

"Whatever you guys decide to do, just be careful," Will said. "I know you've been fortunate in these parts, but you gotta remember what kind of world is out there."

"Don't you worry, we'll be very careful," Larry said. He pointed his thumb over his shoulder, toward the open door of the cabin. "I'm gonna go inside and see how Marie is doing on those pancakes."

As Larry disappeared into the smell of sweet carbohydrates, Will turned his attention to Dylan and Mary Beth.

"Do you guys have to go?" Mary Beth asked. "I don't want to stay here without y'all."

Holly said, "Sweetie, we—"

"Yes," Dylan interrupted. "They have to go."

"It's just for the day," Will said, hoping he wasn't

inadvertently lying. "We'll be back before the sun goes down."

Mary Beth said, "Promise?"

Smiling, Will said, "Promise."

Holly leaned down to hug Mary Beth, and Will did the same with the boy.

"You shouldn't make promises you can't keep," Dylan said into Will's ear.

Will pulled away from Dylan, placing his hands on each of the boy's shoulders.

"I know you're upset," Will said.

"Then why are you leaving?"

"Because we have to."

"Take me with you," Dylan said.

Will sighed. "We can't."

Dylan crossed his arms and stared down at the ground.

"We *will* be back. Alright? Don't you worry about it." Will nodded toward Mary Beth. "Just take care of her, okay?"

Continuing to stare at the ground, Dylan nodded.

Holly stood up and looked as if she was about to cry, and Will used his eyes to tell her to keep it together. They had to stay strong for the children. Holly nodded, and managed to keep from showing her emotion.

"You guys all set?" Charlie's voice came from across the grounds, where the vehicles were parked.

"Coming," Will said back. He looked over to Holly and signaled her on.

On his way down the stairs, Will looked back to Dylan. Will smiled, then looked to Mary Beth.

"Don't let him get upset when you catch more fish than him," Will said.

This brought a smile out of both the kids, which made Will

happy as he turned away from them and joined Charlie at the van.

***

The sun had dried most of the mud, making the drive down the mountain less treacherous. Few clouds spread across the eastern horizon, telling Will that they might have a clear day ahead of them.

They reached the bottom of the mountain, turning onto the familiar stretch of interstate. Charlie had opted to drive, knowing the lay of the land much better than either Will or Holly.

"You definitely know where you're going?" Holly asked from the back seat.

"For sure," Charlie said. "I had some buddies who went to UNC, and we'd occasionally ride up to Durham from Chapel Hill to go to this bar we really liked. It should only take us a couple of hours to get there."

"If we're lucky," Will said.

They drove past the camping store, and Will looked down to see dozens of the monsters loitering in the parking lot. He wondered if the creatures had been out there waiting for him, Charlie, and Scott to return.

As they passed the Outdoors Unlimited exit, Charlie said, "Well, this is officially the furthest I've gone since this all started. I'm not gonna lie to you, it's kinda nice to get out for a while."

"Believe me," Will said, "you should be counting your blessings that you haven't had to be out on the open road."

Will could feel Charlie take his eyes off the road to glance over toward him, but Charlie never spoke about it. Instead, he changed the subject.

"So, I never did ask. How did you two meet?"

Holly leaned up between the seats and said, "I kidnapped him."

Charlie laughed, and it even made Will smile.

"That's funny. But really, how did y'all meet?"

Will took his focus off the empty pastures to turn to Charlie. He said, "She kidnapped me."

Charlie furrowed his brow. "Seriously?"

Will didn't really want to hear the story, but Holly told it anyway. There was nothing he wanted to hear about less than David Ellis, but he understood that Charlie would just prod them until one of them explained, so he did his best to watch the passing scenes outside and ignore what she was saying. It would've been a good time to have his smartphone so he could blast a heavy metal record in his ears or listen to The Joe Rogan Podcast. *To only be afforded such luxuries,* he thought.

"Well, ain't that a backwards ass way to fall in love?" Charlie said.

Will felt a hand clutch his shoulder, and turned to see Holly's beautiful green eyes staring at him. She leaned forward and kissed him, then ducked back into the back seat.

"Oh, shit," Charlie said.

Will looked ahead to see a group of Empties lumbering along in the middle of the road. This had been a common occurrence on their travels, and he was honestly surprised this was the first horde they'd seen on the short trip.

"This is gonna happen a lot," Holly said. "You've just got to drive around them."

"We'll have to take each of these scenarios on a case by case basis," Will said. "If there's no way around, we'll have to clear 'em out ourselves."

This group gathered around only one abandoned car, leaving an entire two lanes of interstate wide open. Charlie veered away from the creatures, driving past with the vehicle unscathed. The beasts hissed and growled as the van rode by, but they became but a speck in the mirrors in no time.

"I hope it's that easy every time," Charlie said.

Will forced a short laugh. "Yeah, me too."

***

In just a hair over three hours, they reached Durham. Being naive and somewhat ignorant to what it was really like out on the interstates, Charlie had calculated their ETA as if they'd be driving 70 or 80 MPH the entire way. He hadn't accounted for how often they'd have to slow down to 20 or 30 in order to maneuver around a group of Empties, or collections of abandoned cars. Luckily, they'd only been forced to get out of the vehicle one time to take out a small horde of the creatures. All told, it had added just under an hour to his original projections.

The church itself actually sat on the outskirts of Durham, meaning they didn't have to drive all the way into the city. Will was surprised to find the church standing all on its own, with no other structures in the vicinity. It was the only building off of the exit, and he'd known they were approaching it from miles away, upon seeing the three large crosses on the horizon, the one in the middle being slightly taller than the others. He'd seen these sorts of mega-churches before. He specifically remembered passing by one in Memphis that was very similar, just off Interstate 40.

"A church this big, do you think there will be survivors here?" Will pondered. "Seems like it would be a pretty common place for people to migrate to in such a disaster."

"Very possible," Charlie said. "If that ends up being the case, we need to be very careful about who we share the information we have with. Don't know what kind of panic that could cause."

"Agreed," Will said.

Charlie pulled onto the exit ramp and took a left at the end of it. They crossed over the bridge, and Will looked down the way they'd come to see the tops of all the abandoned vehicles. A group of Empties they'd just passed about a quarter of a mile back limped down the highway, following the same path they'd taken, as if the creatures actually thought they'd catch the van. As far as Will knew, the things didn't possess the ability for thought. They didn't have feelings or the ability to convey emotions. They walked and they ate, until they were destroyed. That was it.

Around twenty cars remained in the parking lot, most of them parked in spaces. Two vehicles had collided near the middle of the lot, and sat with doors open, the cars' front ends still mended together. Near the two wrecked vehicles lay the remains of five dead bodies, two of which had been children. Will swallowed the lump in his throat.

"Guys," Holly said, pointing toward the front of the church.

The front entrance to the church, guarded with two engraved, wooden doors, was wide open. Large, stained glass windows were up high on the side of the building, bringing the sunlight into its large sanctuary.

"You think any of those things are inside?" Charlie asked.

"If there were any in the parking lot, then you can be damn sure they're now inside," Will said.

"I think that's the library over there," Charlie said, pointing to a wing of the building. The mega-church was made up of only one structure, so if there were Empties inside, they could be anywhere.

"Looks like there is a door leading straight into that part of the building," Holly said. "We should go check and see if it's unlocked."

Will reached into one of the duffle bags, pulling out a pair of flashlights. He handed one of the lights to Charlie and kept one for himself.

"Let's go check it out," Will said.

CHAPTER TWENTY

Even though it was a church, Will was still surprised when the side entrance of the place was unlocked, opening without a fight. They entered the building, unable to see with the power out. The sun brought at least some light in through the door — enough for them to see that they were, indeed, inside a library. Will clicked on his flashlight. He'd brought with him a rifle, which hung over his shoulder, as well as a pistol. A knife hung next to the sidearm, along with a pouch containing extra ammunition. Behind him, Charlie clicked on the other flashlight.

"Stay close," Will whispered. He then stood still, trying to see if he could hear any of the creatures inside of the building. It was quiet as he took the first step into the building.

With the sun pounding the opposite side of the church, the natural light quickly dissipated. Three tables sat just in front of them, each with four chairs neatly pushed under them. Beyond those tables started the rows of shelves housing books. It didn't appear to be as large as the local public libraries that Will had visited countless times. He'd become somewhat of a bibliophile in his late twenties, so he'd spent quite a lot of time in libraries. Not that any of that mattered now.

"How the hell are we supposed to find what we're looking for with no light?" Holly asked.

"Just check as many books as you can," Will said. "You two check out these racks." He was signaling to the bookshelves just in front of them. "I'm gonna head over to the other side of the room and see what I can find."

"Be careful," Holly said.

"Likewise," Will said.

He moved slowly, listening carefully for Empties. The wide open doors at the sanctuary entrance of the church weighed heavy on his mind. There were a few cars in the parking lot, so there was a good chance that someone had been here at the time of The Fall.

When he reached the shelves on the other side of the room, he began to run the light across each row of books, observing each spine as quickly as possible. In truth, he wasn't sure what exactly he was looking for. But he searched for words and phrases like: exorcism, lost testament, lost books of The Bible, the truth about Revelation, demons - anything that could possibly relate to the widespread demon possession that had seemingly infected the world.

After a few minutes of searching, Charlie whispered from the other side of the room, "Any luck?"

"No," Will said. He refocused on the shelves, shining the light on the books that lay in front of him.

Will jerked his head when he heard a groan. He stood completely still, listening to make sure he wasn't just hearing things. He looked over to where Holly and Charlie stood, noticing Holly's flashlight had become still. They'd apparently heard the noise, as well.

The noise happened again. No doubt now that it had been a groan, but it was hard to tell if it was that of a human or that of the possessed. He began moving toward the far end of the aisle he stood in, hoping to creep around and sneak up on the sound. He hated that he had to use a flashlight. If someone was waiting on him, they would sure have the upper hand.

He came to a wall and flashed his light onto a doorway about ten feet from where he stood. He heard the groan again. It sounded as if it may have been coming through the door. His back to the wall, Will looked over to see that Holly and Charlie hadn't moved. Holly held the flashlight now. The light from it reflected off Holly's face, and Will could see the concern in it. Will put his finger to his lips, signaling to Holly to be quiet. He poked his head into the doorway, and heard the moan again. It was definitely the moan of a man, not a beast. Will pointed the flashlight into the room, and a man sitting in the corner of the tiny space covered his face.

"Please," the man said. "Don't hurt me."

Will looked over toward Charlie and Holly and said, "Guys, come here. I found someone," and the two of them hurried over.

"I beg you," the man said. "Please, don't hurt me."

"I'm not going to hurt you," Will said. "I want to help you."

"I am afraid, son, that I am not to be helped." The man put out his arm, revealing a nasty bite, just as Holly and Charlie arrived behind him.

"Shit," Holly mumbled.

Will pointed his light at the man, who covered his face again, pleading for Will to turn the light away. The man wore a white cloak, with almost matching hair on the top of his head. He was a priest. Will hurried to the man's side and kneeled down next to him.

"Please, stay back," the priest said.

Will shined his light on the man's body, noticing that one of his hands clutched his opposite leg. The priest pulled the hand away, revealing a large wound where a chunk had been taken out of his calf. He'd been bitten.

A thunderous bang out in the library pulled Will's attention away from the priest. Charlie grabbed the flashlight from Holly and darted out into the main room.

"They're coming," the priest said.

Will furrowed his brow. "Who? Who's coming?"

"The demon people," the priest said.

Will's eyes widened. "Demons?"

Charlie returned and said, "We gotta get the hell out of here. A bunch of those things are about to bust down a door and fill this library."

"Help me get him up," Will said.

"Will," Holly said, "he's been bitten. We can't help him."

"I think he knows something about the possessions," Will said. "Just help me get him out of here."

The priest wasn't obese by any means, but he'd possibly taken communion a time or two too many. Will lifted up under one arm while Charlie propped the priest up under the other. Holly stationed herself just outside of the room, keeping one of the flashlights focused inside the room to give the men light, while keeping the other on the door being beaten at by the creatures.

Both Will and Charlie groaned as they got the priest up onto his feet. The priest cried out as his weight fell onto his wounded leg.

"We've gotta hurry," Holly said. "They're coming."

The three men hobbled out of the room, the old priest breathing heavily as they moved. He began to mumble something that Will couldn't quite make out. Will didn't know how long it'd been since the priest had been bitten, but he knew the demon was burying itself deep inside of the man's mind. If they hoped to get any information out of this man of God, they'd have to hurry.

Nervous and terrified, Holly had moved too far in front of the three men, taking all the light with her. Right as Will was about to call out to her to slow down, Charlie tripped over the leg of a chair and all three men tumbled to the ground. When the priest screamed, the Empties seemed to bang against the door even harder. Will heard the sound of splintering wood.

"Holly, help us!" Will yelled.

Charlie groaned and cried out, as he'd initiated the fall, and most of the priest's heavy frame had fallen onto him. Will got to his knees, and he and Holly rolled the preacher's weight off of Charlie. The three of them stood the priest back up, and the two men assumed their positions beside him.

Will said to Holly, "Stay focused. We need light to guide us out of here."

She nodded, her hand trembling, obviously regretful of her mistake. They were halfway to the exit when the door crashed open. Holly shone the light in that direction, revealing the faces of an undead onslaught headed for them.

"Move!" Will shouted.

They began to trudge toward the door again, Holly staying only a few feet in front of them now. She pocketed one of the flashlights, and withdrew her sidearm. For once, the creatures had an advantage in speed. Will had to dig down deep in order to move the priest with haste, and Charlie walked with a limp now from their fall. Holly moved ahead of them enough to push a table out of the way, creating a clear path. The Empties moved down a nearby aisle of bookshelves, almost as if they were looking to cut them off.

Holly reached the door first, the three men cutting the distance down as quick as they could.

The first gunshot went off as Holly pointed the light toward the oncoming creatures. One of them had gotten too close for comfort, and she fired off another round, sending the thing to the ground with a snarl. She opened the door, bringing in natural light.

"Hurry," she yelled, firing off a third shot.

The three men made it to the door, and when they were outside, Will pulled away, and both men fell to the ground. He withdrew his pistol, turned, and fired through the door.

"Come on!" he shouted to Holly.

Holly turned and came outside, just as one of the creatures lunged at her. Will aimed the gun past her, and put a bullet into the thing's head. He went to pull the door shut and it slammed on one of the creature's hands.

"Shit!"

He went to shoot the hand, but dropped his gun from his trembling grip. Will stood at an angle, where Holly couldn't get a shot off, so he drew his knife from his side. With a thunderous cry, he drove the sharp tip of the knife down into the thing's hand. With no apparent sense of pain, the strike didn't seem to faze the creature. Will stabbed again, and again, carving away flesh with each blow, until the thing's hand finally disappeared. Will managed to get the door shut just as another hand was about to wedge it open. He fell to the ground, his back against the door, and breathed heavy.

"Holy shit," Charlie said, working to catch his own breath. He rolled onto his back, his stomach rising and falling.

Will jumped when the creatures inside began to bang against the door. He knew from experience that they'd have to open the door on accident in order to get outside without breaking the door down. Either way, their time was short.

Lying on his side and clutching his stomach with one hand, the priest gasped for air. His other hand comforted the wound on his leg. Will hurried to his side, and rolled the man onto his stomach. The priest's pupils had turned pale, and he gurgled as he breathed.

"Back there, you said 'demon'," Will said. "Do you know about the possessions?"

"Possessions?" the priest mumbled.

Will rolled up his shirt sleeve, revealing his wounds. "I was bitten, and the only reason I survived was because a man, a preacher like yourself, performed some sort of an exorcism on me. He drew a demon out of me. That's what's infecting these things."

The man's fading eyes went wide.

"That's why we came here," Will continued. "To try and find some answers in one of the books in there."

"Oh my," the man said. "H-h-he was right."

Will narrowed his eyes. "Who? Who was right?"

"Y-You." The priest coughed. It went on for a time, and Will thought he would lose the man before he could speak again. But the man found his breath and was able to stop coughing. "You must travel to Roanoke. There, you will meet a man. His name is Philip. Father Philip Bartman. Tell him Father Bryant sent you. He will have the answers you seek."

"How do you know he's still alive?" Will asked.

"He will be," Father Bryant said. "He has been waiting."

"Waiting for what? Where will we find him?" Will asked. He had so many questions. Far more questions than he had time. Father Bryant reached out and grabbed onto Will's arm, wrapping it with a blood-stained handprint.

"P-p-please. Do not let me turn. Promise me that you will not let me turn."

"Wait," Will said.

The priest used what felt like all his remaining strength to squeeze Will's arm and repeated himself. "Promise me."

"I promise," Will mumbled. He looked back to Holly, who had tears in her eyes. Charlie stood just behind her, listening in close. He glanced back down to the preacher and took his hand. "*We* promise."

Father Bryant forced his mouth into a small grin. Then his head fell to the side, eyes wide open, and he was gone.

The creatures continued to bang at the door. Charlie looked around the corner to the front of the building.

"More of those things coming out of the front door," Charlie said. "We've gotta go."

Will looked back to Holly and said, "Go to the truck. Both of you. Get it started." He then refocused his attention on Father Bryant as Holly's crying faded toward the SUV.

"I'm not sure how much more of this I can take," Will said, speaking low to himself. "This much death. This much killing." He pulled out his knife, its blade still covered in blood from the beast's hand on the door. He pressed the tip of the knife against the preacher's temple.

"Forgive me, Lord."

CHAPTER TWENTY-ONE

They headed back to the cabins with more than enough daylight left. They'd anticipated being at the church much longer, looking through books. If there was one thing Will had been taught over and over again over the last couple of weeks, though, it had been that life was unpredictable.

"We're going, aren't we?" Holly said, speaking of Roanoke and the man that Father Bryant had told them about.

"I don't know," Will said.

"I can see it in your eyes that you want to go," Holly said.

Holly sat in the back seat, and Will turned to face her.

How can we not go?" Will asked.

"We decided to stay at the camp so we wouldn't have to do this kinda stuff any longer," Holly said. "Now, you're talking about driving to another state. This trip was one thing, being only a couple of hours. But Virginia would keep us out for more than a day."

"Guys," Charlie said. "We don't have to make any decisions now, right? Let's just cool off and think about it later."

Sighing, Will turned back and watched the scenery outside pass by. They drove through a rural area, nothing but pasture and billboards every way that he looked. Holly had read him correctly in thinking that he wanted to seek out the priest in Roanoke. Will had died, which was something that, no matter how hard she tried, Holly just couldn't understand. And for whatever reason, he'd been saved. Was he part of some bigger plan? Or was it just dumb fucking luck that he'd happened to have been around Samuel when he'd been bit? Without thinking much of it, he rubbed the wounds on his arm over his shirt. It had become a sort of habit, and he'd do it without being fully aware that he was doing so.

For now, all he really wanted was to get back to the campground. He wanted to eat and he wanted to sleep.

The decision on Roanoke could wait.

***

From the moment they reached the exit to the cabins, something didn't feel right. It was almost as if trouble lurked in the air, and Will inhaled it. He'd remained quiet for the duration of the trip, ever since he and Holly had had a short argument. She'd stayed quiet, as well, sitting in the back seat with her arms crossed.

Charlie turned onto the road that led up the mountain to the cabins, and everything looked just as it had when they'd left. Will laughed in his mind at his own paranoia. He still needed sleep, but now, with the possible impending trip to Roanoke, he wasn't sure if he'd get a break at all. If they were going to make the trip, they'd need to just go. What if Father Bartman was there now, but planning his own exit? Or, what if they got there, and he'd suffered the same fate as the preacher from the library? They couldn't afford to wait.

"What the— " Charlie said.

Will looked up and wiped his eyes, having almost faded off to sleep. When they were clear, he saw the smoke on the horizon. It rose from the exact spot that the cabins were located. Holly leaned in between the front seats, getting her own look at the hazy skyline.

"Larry or someone must've started a fire pit outside," Holly said.

Charlie shook his head. "No, we never start them this early. It's the middle of the afternoon and it's not even that chilly outside. We usually get the fire going about half an hour before the sun starts to go down. This isn't right."

Will could see in Charlie's eyes that something was wrong. He felt the vehicle accelerate. The engine whined. Will wanted to urge Charlie to slow down and be careful, worried that he may be losing his intuition, but instead, Will turned to Holly.

"Check our arms and make sure they're loaded. Hand me my rifle once you're done."

Will reached to his side and drew his sidearm. He checked the clip, assuring himself that it was full. He could hear the clicking in the back seat of Holly checking their other guns, and after a moment, she handed Will the rifle, and extra ammunition for both it and his sidearm. He was looking down, quadruple checking his gear, when the vehicle came to a stop. Holly gasped, sounding as if her hand had covered her mouth.

Will looked up.

Larry and Marie's cabin was on fire.

***

What looked to be about fifteen Empties, at minimum, loitered around the courtyard.

Will looked over to Charlie in the driver's seat, whose face had gone blank. Charlie stared up at the cabins, his hands gripping the wheel tight. Just as Will was about to try and snap Charlie out of it, Charlie's eyes narrowed into anger, and he slammed his foot down onto the gas. Will's head jerked back into the headrest, and Charlie used every ounce of the V8 engine to race toward the creatures.

"Slow down!" Will yelled.

But Charlie seemed to blank out all the noise around him. He ignored Will, and kept the truck aimed like a weapon at the Empties. Charlie wasn't going to stop. Will only hoped that none of the other survivors were trapped among the horde, what with the truck coming toward it like a bullet.

"Shit! Hold on!" Will yelled back to Holly.

Charlie screamed.

The truck barreled into the horde like a bowling bowl rolling a perfect strike. Countless creatures bounced off the hood and the windshield. The glass cracked, and Will put his hands up, as if that would protect him if any of the Empties came through the thick windshield.

Charlie slammed on the breaks, and the car's tires fishtailed in the gravel. It came to a stop near the playground, and Will saw another small horde near the woods, heading toward the camp. He looked toward the courtyard. The truck had taken out the majority of that group, but about seven Empties still stood.

"Come on!" Will shouted. He opened the door and stepped out of the truck. He put the rifle to his shoulder, aimed at the first Empty in the courtyard, and fired. He missed the one he had been aiming at, instead sending a round into the chest of one of the undead beings behind it.

"Charlie!"

Will looked back inside the truck to see Holly reaching into the front seat, trying to hand Charlie a gun. Charlie wouldn't accept it, a dazed look of shock on his face as he stared off ahead.

Will raced around the front end of the car and swung open Charlie's door.

"Charlie, snap the fuck out of it! We need you!"

Charlie sat there, his mouth wide open, staring off into the woods, apparently looking past the oncoming group of Empties.

Will turned and aimed his rifle toward the horde coming from the woods.

"Holly," Will shouted, "I need you!" He fired, missing his target again and sending the bullet sailing past the entire group.

Holly opened the door and jumped out of the truck. Will looked back inside, and Charlie was looking toward him. The second gunshot, sounding off near Charlie's head, must've snapped him out of his trance. Will reached into the truck and grabbed Charlie by the collar.

"I need you," Will said. "If you want *any* chance of saving these people, get your ass out here and fight."

Charlie hesitantly nodded. He then reached onto the passenger seat and grabbed the gun Holly had left for him. He stepped out of the truck, and aimed at the horde coming out of the woods.

"Stay with him," Will told Holly. He hurried to the other side of the truck, and took aim at the group of Empties in the courtyard. They had closed the distance halfway on the truck, allowing Will a much better chance of hitting his targets. He took aim, and fired.

Will took down two of the creatures before he was forced to reload again. Every time one of the beasts fell, it was almost as if the others became more motivated to get to him.

"Talk to me," Will said, reloading his rifle and stepping back toward the truck. "How're y'all doing?"

"It looks like there's just more coming," Holly said.

Will shot down two more Empties down before his back hit the truck. His rifle ran out of ammunition again, but he didn't have the time to reload. Instead, he tossed the rifle over his shoulder and drew his handgun. One of the thing's lunged at him, and he pulled the gun up just in time to hit the Empty square in the forehead. He then raced around the back of the truck, joining Charlie and Holly.

"Shit," Will said, looking off into the woods. Many bodies lay on the ground, but there were more coming, just as Holly had said. He heard a snarl from behind him. The two remaining Empties from the courtyard had followed him around the truck, and he'd been so distracted by the group near the woods that he'd almost forgotten about them. He fired off two consecutive shots with the handgun, connecting with head shots to both of the creatures.

"We can't take all these things out," Will said. "We've gotta make a run for the cabin."

"It's burning to the ground," Holly said. "How're we supposed to get in there?"

Will shook his head. "I don't know, but we've gotta try. Come on."

Will ducked into the back seat of the vehicle and grabbed their bags. He handed some of the gear over to Charlie and Holly, gathered what he could, and then shut the door and headed around the back of the vehicle, starting toward the cabin.

When they'd made it halfway across the courtyard, a guttural scream came out of the burning cabin. It was the scream of a man. It stopped Will dead in his tracks.

Charlie's jaw dropped open and Holly gasped. A figure come running out the front door. He screamed, like a man, not like one of the creatures, and he was on fire. The man was tall, and wore overalls.

"Oh my God," Charlie said, taking another step toward the burning cabin. "Larry."

Will wrapped his arms around Charlie, who'd started to cry

and yell out, wanting desperately to run to Larry. It took everything Will had to hold him back.

"It's too late," Will said. "We can't help him."

The flaming figure fell face-first onto the grass in front of the cabin. The flames shooting off his body licked the open air, and the person no longer screamed.

Two more figures came through the front door of the cabin, these lumbering with the same gait as the undead. They were Empties, on fire, and apparently unfazed by their flames. Meanwhile, the horde from the woods were quickly approaching the survivors.

"We've gotta move, now," Holly said.

"We've gotta run to our cabin," Will said.

"What about the kids?" Holly asked.

"We'll never make it inside there. His arms wrapped around Charlie's waist, Will pulled back on Charlie. "Come on, man."

Still weeping, Charlie turned and grabbed Will's shirt. Will backed up, and aimed his pistol at the approaching group of Empties and fired.

"Go!" Will shouted at Holly. Charlie pulled away from Will, and both men jogged to the cabin.

When they climbed up the steps, Holly had already opened the front door. Charlie went inside first, and Will stood at the edge of the cabin. He pulled the rifle off his shoulder, reloaded, and aimed down at the horde. He hadn't known Larry that well, but he was tired of seeing good people die from these demons. He fired into the group, again and again. Squeezing the trigger and watching the creatures fall felt good. Every single one of these things deserved to fall. Every one.

"Will!" Holly shouted.

He looked back to her, seeing the worry in her face. The

horde moved only about fifteen yards from the cabin now, and four more had come out of the flaming cabin, all of them on fire. Will took one more shot as he backed up, connecting with his target's skull.

Then he disappeared inside the cabin.

CHAPTER TWENTY-TWO

Will locked the door and dropped his bag in the middle of the floor. Holly searched the cabin for the children. When she returned to the living room, concern spread across her face.

"Not here?" Will asked, speaking of the children.

Holly wiped at her eyes and shook her head.

"Son of a bitch," Will mumbled.

The sound of marching thundered on the front porch, and the Empties banged on the door. Over and over, they slammed their decrepit hands against the front of the cabin, clogging Will's ability to think.

"We can't stay here," Holly said.

"I know," Will said. He ran his hands through his hair, gripping it tight. "Maybe we can get out the back door, and have a clear shot to the car with—" Will stopped himself, realizing what he was suggesting.

"We can't leave," Charlie said. "There could be others."

The banging continued on the front of the cabin, and there were now creatures banging on the windows.

"I know, I know," Will said. He looked at Charlie and said, "You got any ideas?"

An orange glow appeared at the front of the cabin. Two of the burning Empties had made it up the steps. Just outside the window, Will got a good look at them. All their flesh was burned, leaving nothing but flaming statues of muscle and bone. Yet, somehow, the things still were able to move.

"Oh, shit," Will said.

The flames licked the roof of the log cabin's porch, catching it on fire.

Holly put her hands on top of her head, showing her panic. She started to pace and curse under her breath. The glass of the window broke from all the pressure, and Will readied his gun.

"Grab your weapons!" Will yelled. He fired, taking out the creature whose face filled the window.

The horde filled most of the front porch. As they fired at the creatures, Will could see the door start to give way on its hinges. Flames swam in through the window, threatening to catch the kitchen on fire. Staying in the middle of the cabin would soon no longer be an option. He brought down another creature with a bullet, then started to back up as he reloaded.

"We've gotta move," Will said. He grabbed ahold of Holly's arm and started for the rear of the cabin. Charlie ran ahead of them, opening the door to the master bedroom. All three loaded inside the room, and Will shut and locked the door.

"What the hell are we supposed to do?" Charlie asked. "Either they're gonna break in here, or this place is gonna burn to the fucking ground." The smoke had begun to reek throughout the entire cabin. They had little time.

Will said to Holly, "Grab your essentials. We're gonna have to sneak out the back door."

As Will and Holly began gathering their things, the continuous banging at the front of the cabin stopped. His hands still in his bag, Will turned and looked back toward the door.

"They stopped," Holly said.

Will said, "Shh," putting his index finger to his lip. He was pretty sure he heard something past the crackling of the flames and the muffled snarls of the creatures. It sounded like the voice of a human.

Charlie was the first one to say, "What the hell?"

Someone whistling. Someone calling out, "Over here!"

Will looked out a window, through the flames. The fire had made it into the kitchen, but the Empties had retreated from the porch. Will squinted his eyes, looking through the mirage of smoke to see someone jumping up and down across the courtyard, waving their arms.

"Scott!" Charlie said.

"Quiet," Will said. "He's drawing them over to him so we can get the hell out of here."

Will retreated back into the bedroom and grabbed his things. He threw on the rifle, feeling the strap rub against his neck. He picked up Holly's bag, too, and then he returned to the living room and handed it to her.

"I want you to go out the back with Charlie," Will said. "When you get down to the end of this row of cabins, drop your bag. You two head back to the truck, using it as cover, and flank them from the front."

"What are you gonna do?" Holly asked.

"I'm gonna go out the front door."

"No," Holly said. "You can't go out there alone. Besides, you'll get burned."

Will said, "I'll be fine. There's still time for me to make it out. With you guys distracting them, they'll be halfway across the courtyard once I get outside. I'm gonna take as many of them out from behind as I can and draw them away from Scott. You guys should be around the other side of them by the time that happens, and you'll have an opening. There aren't that many of them. We should be able to make this work. But we don't have a lot of time, so you've gotta go."

Holly's face told Will everything he needed to know. She

didn't like the plan. Didn't want to leave Will's side. But they didn't have a choice. They couldn't stay here, and Scott had given them the opening they needed.

Charlie grabbed onto Holly's arm and began to pull her. She held her ground, leaning into Will to kiss him on the lips.

He said, "I'll see you in a few minutes."

Will pulled away from her, and headed for the front door. When he turned around again, Charlie and Holly had disappeared to the back of the cabin. The fire had made it into the kitchen, lighting the cabinets aflame. Will thought to salvage any food or medical supplies he could get, but there wasn't time. The number one focus right now was to clear out this band of creatures so that they could look for Dylan and Mary Beth, and then they'd be able to regroup and inventory all their supplies from the other cabins.

Will went to open the door, but quickly drew his hand away from the metal handle. It was hot.

"Son of a bitch."

He waved his hand, hoping to bring relief and to cool down the burn. He also started to cough, the smoke quickly filling the cabin. He glanced out the window, seeing that Scott was now having to back up towards the woods, the creatures gaining on him.

Will stepped back from the door. He counted down from three, then picked up his leg and slammed his foot into the front door. As soon as he connected, he turned his back to the adjacent wall, clearing the path of the entrance. The door opened with a 'woosh', and flames came spilling into the cabin, like pouring lighter fluid over a charcoal grill. The backdraft wasn't as strong as he'd anticipated, but it had been enough to where it would've set him on fire if he hadn't moved out of the way.

After the fire dissipated, Will came off the wall and turned out of the door. Flames engulfed the porch, forcing him to run through a shallow fire, then jump down the three stairs leading to the concrete. The heavy bag on his shoulder, he fell to the ground, his ankle twisting. He landed on the bag, knocking the breath out of his lungs as his ribs slammed into it. He writhed on the ground, safe from the flames, but unsure whether to grab his aching ribs or to clutch his throbbing ankle. He found the sense to look up. He'd apparently made enough noise to lure at least a small population of the Empties back toward him, thus ruining his idea of a surprise attack.

Breathing heavily now that he lay in the fresh, open air, away from the toxic smoke, he tried to make it to his feet, but fell down again when he attempted to put weight on his ankle. From the angle he lay at, he couldn't see Scott beyond the swarm of Empties. He glanced toward the vehicle, not seeing Charlie or Holly. They should've been there by now, and he hadn't heard any gunshots come from the rear of the cabin. With no other choice, he drew his pistol and fired at the creatures coming toward him.

They moved slow enough and were far enough away where he could take his time and make each shot count. There were only four of the beasts coming toward him, but the shots would sure garner the attention of others. He took aim and fired. The first shot missed his target, but he quickly shot again, taking down the first Empty. He shot again, nicking the neck of the next creature. They had cut the distance on him in half, and if he couldn't make it to his feet, he knew he might not survive. Will got up to his knees, at least allowing himself to aim better. He shot the Empty he'd grazed again, this time hitting it in the face.

When he aimed at the next beast, the gun clicked.

"Shit!"

He went for his pouch, then quickly adjusted and grabbed his knife instead. Mouth open, the Empty lunged at him. With a yell, Will drew the knife and jammed it into the side of the creature's head as all its weight fell onto Will. He groaned as the lifeless thing fell onto his aching ribs. He was unable to muster the energy to get the thing off of him. Will lifted his head, and saw more of the creatures heading his way. He mustered every ounce of energy he had, but couldn't get the creature off of him. In its human days, the thing had been a heavy-set woman, around 240 pounds — far too heavy for him to push her off of him with his injuries.

"Help!" Will finally called, with no other choice. He could feel the pain in his gut as he called out, like someone grinding their fist into his injured ribs as he pushed the cry out through his lungs. He knew that yelling would likely bring the whole group toward him, but it wouldn't matter if the monsters already headed his way made it over to him.

"Help! Holly!" This time when he yelled, he used everything he had left in him. He cried louder, sounding more desperate. He picked his head up again, and could now see more of the creatures coming his way. He tried again to lift the hunk of dead weight from on top of him, but failed, yet again. He found himself confused, not sure what had happened to Holly, Charlie, and Scott. Had they run into resistance behind the cabins?

Will tried to ready his knife for the oncoming gang, but it was still lodged in the skull of the body on top of him, and his arm was pinned.

"Fuck!"

He looked up again, and the swarm was almost close enough

now to where they could spit on him. Will made one last effort at his knife, and he shifted the weight of the beast further onto his arm. He yelled out, feeling that if he moved anymore, his arm might snap. An Empty had started to lean down to come for him when the first new shot sounded off through the air, and half of the creature's head disappeared. Its limp body collapsed just a few feet away from Will. Human screams sounded across the campground, and the onslaught began.

One by one, the creatures fell. They'd turned their attention away from Will, and he followed their gaze to see Holly, Charlie, and Scott, weapons in hand, each mowing through the mob of Empties with gunpowder and lead. Will heard several bullets whistling overhead, missing their targets.

Another creature approached, kicking gravel and snarling. It was about to lunge at Will when it fell like its counterpart had just moments earlier. A shadow came over Will, and Holly was there. Gunshots continued in the background as she leaned down and rolled the dead, overweight beast off of him.

"Come on," she said, grabbing his arm.

"Wait," he said, pleading. "You're gonna have to help me. I twisted my ankle, and I'm not sure if I broke a rib or not."

Holly squatted down, and Will got up onto his knees. It felt like a shank jabbing into his side, but he got his arm around her, and used his good leg to stand up. Charlie and Scott provided cover fire for them as Will hobbled on his decent leg, on their way over to the van.

"Get him in the van!" Charlie said. "We can finish them off!"

Holly opened the sliding door, and she and Will loaded into the van. He felt safe to be inside the vehicle, the ringing in his ears only making it harder to handle the pain in his ankle and in his mid-section.

"Are you okay?" Holly asked.

Will nodded. "I'll be fine."

Moments later, the gunshots ceased. Charlie squatted down, fighting to catch his breath. Scott, seemingly in shock from what had happened, dropped the rifle he'd been firing and put his arms behind his head. He began to pace in circles, disoriented and confused about what was happening. Holly opened the door to the van, and Charlie straightened and joined she and Will.

"You alright?" Charlie asked Will.

Clutching onto his ribs, Will asked, "What the hell happened to y'all?"

"We got caught behind the cabin with four Empties," Holly said. "One of them attacked Charlie, and I thought he got bit."

"Shook me up real bad," Charlie said.

"We didn't use our guns because we didn't want to ruin your ambush on this group," Holly continued. She smiled and said, "Looks like you didn't need us for that," making light of the situation.

Will ignored Holly's attempt at humor, looking past her to glance at Scott. He seemed short on breath, hyperventilating. His hands remained behind his head, continuing to show him in an utter state of panic and confusion. Will slid off the seat and onto the gravel. His ankle felt better, but he still used Charlie and Holly to stand, and applied all his weight to his healthy leg.

"Scott," Will said. At first, Scott didn't move. He just continued looking forward, spots of blood splattered on his white shirt. Will called his name again, louder this time. It garnered Scott's attention, and he turned.

Will let go of Charlie and Holly, and took a step. Holly joined arms with him, which he allowed even though he was now able to put some weight on his leg. No reason to get too confident and hurt it even more.

Scott's breathing sounded like that of a terrified child. His eyes were wide and bloodshot, and he looked like he'd seen a ghost — which really wasn't far from the truth.

"Scott," Will said, "what happened?"

Scott shuddered, still not snapping out of his shock and fear.

"Scott!" Will said.

Holly put her hand on Will's shoulder, and looked at him, shaking her head. She stepped in between Will and Scott.

"Scott," Holly said softly. "Scott, sweetie."

He gasped, eyes still wide, and looked at Holly. Blood from one of the creatures he'd slain ran down his cheek.

"What happened?" Holly asked, still speaking in the same, mellow tone.

Scott looked back and forth between the three of them, and Holly continued to try and calm him.

"It's okay, sweetie. Just tell me what happened."

Scott's breathing finally started to level. Holly reached down and grabbed Scott's hand, then nodded at him as a signal to go ahead and talk.

"We-we were all outside," Scott said, nervously. "Larry had the door to their cabin open. Marie wasn't feeling too well, so he'd started a fire, but he also wanted to let some fresh air in for her.

"I decided to go and take a nap. I think I'd only been asleep for ten minutes or so when someone screamed and woke me up. I went to the front window of my cabin and—"

Scott had to stop mid-sentence, as he'd begun to cry. He sniffled, wiping his eyes.

"And, what?" Holly asked. "It's okay, go on."

"Th-they were everywhere. An entire mob of those things

flooded into Larry and Marie's cabin. Larry's gun went off a few times, but then all I heard was screaming and the snarls of those things."

"Jesus Christ," Charlie said.

"I didn't know what to do. I couldn't help them. I had no weapons. There was nothing I could do, I'm telling you."

"The kids," Will said. "Where are the children, Scott?"

Scott shook his head. "I don't know. They were with Larry and Marie when I left them. I'm sorry. I'm so sorry." He was crying, and sounded like he'd mentally lost it. He said, "I can't do this," and cupped the back of his head with his hands again. He paced to the middle of the courtyard, and sat down on top of one of the picnic tables.

Will looked to Charlie and Holly. "We have to check that cabin. The kids could still be inside."

"How are we supposed to get inside? Look at that place," Charlie said.

Holly appeared on the verge of losing her shit in the same way that Scott had. Will gently grabbed her by the forearm and said, "Stay calm. I need you." Holly wiped her eyes and nodded.

Will said, "We've gotta—"

The explosion came out of nowhere. Will threw himself onto Holly, not thinking or caring about the pain in his ankle or his ribs. She screamed, and he covered her head, the boom going off in his ears. Debris fell around them, but they were more than fortunate when only some small scraps of wood fell onto Will's back.

Will poked his head up and looked back to see that Larry and Marie's cabin had exploded. His immediate thoughts went to Dylan, Mary Beth, and Reece. Will removed his weight from Holly, and slowly rose to his knees. He watched what was left of the cabin, still in flames. Holly appeared beside him, weeping.

Will put his arm around her and pulled her close. She sank her head into his chest, and let everything out.

After a few moments spent in shock, Will remembered the others. He turned to the left, looking for Charlie first. Charlie lay on his stomach, remaining still.

"Charlie, you alright?" Will said.

Charlie picked his head up, uncovering it. He looked back to the cabin, standing with his eyes wide and his mouth open.

Holly pulled away from Will's chest and wiped her eyes. She looked off toward the center of the courtyard and asked, "Where's Scott?"

The blast had scattered the picnic tables, and Scott was nowhere to be seen. Will moved Holly away so that he could stand. The adrenaline dissipating, his ribs hurt again, making it difficult to breathe. He gasped, and Holly helped him to his feet.

Charlie moved past them, calling Scott's name.

As Will made it up onto his feet with Holly's assistance, Charlie cried out a four-letter word and raced toward debris. Will followed Charlie's path and saw a leg hanging out from a stack of tangled wood.

"Oh, shit," Will mumbled.

He began to hobble toward the pile, and Holly helped him until Will demanded she leave his side and rush over to help Charlie remove the debris from on top of Scott. Or, at least, what they thought to be Scott.

The body lay under only a couple of layers of light debris, and by the time Will made it over, Charlie and Holly had both turned away, their faces covered. Will slipped between the two of them to look down and see Scott's eyes, wide open. Blood was everywhere, and an indistinguishable piece of metal jutted from his chest, having impaled him.

Will looked away, glancing back to the cabin. The two cabins on either side now stood aflame.

Will grabbed Holly by the hand. "Come on," he said.

Crying, Holly asked, "Where are we going?"

Before Will could answer, from out of the woods they heard a gunshot, followed by the scream of a young girl.

CHAPTER TWENTY-THREE

He stood there, the gun still shaking in his hand. Even though this wasn't the first time he'd destroyed one of the creatures, it may as well have been. It lay on the ground, motionless, the top half of its body sunk under the water on the shore.

Behind Dylan, Mary Beth cried. Her weeping snapped him out of his shock.

Reece sat against a tree, clutching his neck. Blood seeped between his fingers. The creature had just missed the vein bulging from the boy's thin neck. Even with everything Dylan had seen over the past couple of weeks, he'd never seen so much fear in anyone's eyes.

Leaves rustled not too far off through the trees as more of the Empties headed toward them.

"What are we gonna do?" cried Mary Beth.

"Help me get him up," Dylan said.

Dylan had only gotten a few feet away from Reece when the teenager began shaking his head and stuck the palm of his free hand out, telling the two younger kids not to move any closer. Dylan could see under Reece's crimson stained hand just how bad the wound was. The Empty had taken a chunk out of Reece's neck, thus rendering him unable to speak. Even over the sound of the group approaching, Dylan could hear the hiss of the blood seeping from Reece's throat, like a puncture in a running hose.

His lips moved, but no words came out.

"What?" Dylan asked.

Reece reached down and drew something small from his pocket. The black object firm in his hand, he pressed a small button, triggering a blade to appear from the handle. Again, he tried to speak, and again no words came out. But, this time Dylan was able to make out what he was saying.

His lips mouthed one word: "Go."

Mary Beth cried louder, covering her mouth in an attempt to mute herself. Dylan again saw the hurt in Reece's eyes. As young as Dylan was, even he knew that no one deserved to die like this. Especially someone not much older than he himself was. But with the horde fast approaching, Dylan had to honor Reece's wish in order to save himself and Mary Beth.

Dylan slipped the handgun back into his pack, and put his hand on Mary Beth's back. He said, "Let's go. We gotta get out of here."

Pulling her hands away from her face, Mary Beth said, "We can't leave him. I won't let him just sit out here and die alone in the woods."

When Dylan looked back to Reece, he could now see the frustration in his friend's face. He'd told them to go, yet there they stood, wasting time. The group of creatures was getting louder and louder, closer and closer, with each wasted moment that passed.

In one fluid movement, Reece pulled the hand away that was applying pressure to the bite wound. The flesh hung off the teen's neck like the skin of a potato being peeled. Reece mouthed something to himself, though all Dylan could hear were the sniffles of Reece's cries. Reece closed his eyes, and brought the blade to his throat.

Dylan yelled, then thought enough to shield Mary Beth from the gruesome scene, turning away himself at the last moment.

Dylan heard the blade hit the ground, then the sound of Reece's body tumbling over onto its side.

The yell that Dylan bellowed made the volume of the creatures' snarls increase, and when Dylan turned back, it was almost as if the gang was moving faster toward them. He lifted under Mary Beth's arms.

"We gotta go."

She looked up, and he shielded her eyes again before her gaze fell upon Reece's fallen corpse. He guided her past the tree before removing his hand from her face. She started to look back, but he stopped her.

"Don't look," Dylan said. "You don't wanna see it."

Dylan looked back to Reece's folded body lying on its side. The creatures had moved within twenty-five yards of the body. Reece had slit his throat, just trying to end his life. But, as far as Dylan knew, just slicing the throat wouldn't prevent the teenager from becoming one of *them*. He gripped the handle of his own knife, wondering whether he should release Reece by stabbing him in the head. His perspiring hand moistened the grip of his knife. It trembled, and he cried. He couldn't bring himself to further harm his friends' body. He needed to turn his attention to the only thing that mattered — getting himself and Mary Beth to safety.

"Come on," Dylan said, grabbing onto Mary Beth's hand.

And they ran.

They ran as fast as their legs would take them. The overwhelming noise of the herd behind them became softer and softer. They ran until they didn't hear the creatures any longer, glad that they hadn't run into another group. Dylan gasped, trying to catch his breath. He glanced over to the water, but it was gone. He'd completely blanked out while running, and not even realized that they'd moved beyond the large pond. Dylan had planned to use the shoreline to get them back to the cabins.

When he turned around, all he saw were trees. It looked as if someone building the world of a video game had pasted the same row of a hundred trees in, over and over again. Autumn had brought so many leaves down from the branches that there was no way for them to even recover their steps.

They were lost.

Dylan's plan to stay along the shore so that they could use the water to guide them back had failed.

"What are we gonna do?" Mary Beth repeated. Her eyes were barely open, tears streaming down her cheeks. She paced back and forth, shuffling the leaves below her feet. Dylan heard her, but he couldn't tell if it was real or not. Inside, he felt so overwhelmed.

I'm just a kid. I can't take care of us.

Mary Beth continued to plead with him, but he blanked it out.

Dylan fell to his knees, lost in the middle of nowhere. His shoulders shrugged, and he looked down to the ground.

Slowly, he raised his head to the sky. Not even a bird passed through the clouds above. He and Mary Beth were alone. Trapped.

And all he could do was lower his head and cry.

CHAPTER TWENTY-FOUR

As they approached the fishing area, Will found himself nearly out of breath. Behind them, the flames continued breathe into the open sky as the cabins burned to the ground.

The water came into view, and Will came to an abrupt stop as he saw a large group of Empties gathered around a tree. They were focused on something on the ground, each of them either on their knees or bent down. Holly and Charlie had both stopped on either side of Will.

Holly mumbled, "Oh, my God."

The kids, Will thought.

Before either Charlie or Holly could stop him, Will drew his handgun from his hip and ran at the horde.

He screamed, garnering the creatures' attention, and he fired.

Round after round blew from the barrel, until it clicked. He hadn't even bothered to count how many of the things had dropped to the ground. Behind him, Holly and Charlie fired their own weapons. Will grabbed onto the rifle hanging on his shoulder, and began to empty rounds into the creatures.

Everything seemed to slow down around him. It became a blur. He fired the rifle until, like his handgun, it was out of ammunition.

With only one Empty in his sights, Will drew the knife and lunged at the creature. If it had been alive, it likely would have widened its eyes and screamed. Instead, Will bellowed a war cry, blood dripping down his face, and slammed the blade into the side of the thing's head. It fell to the ground, he with it, and Will didn't stop. Over and over, Will jabbed the knife down into the Empty's face. Its features became unrecognizable.

It took Holly screaming at him to finally bring him back to reality.

Will looked back at Holly to see her with tears in her eyes. The look on her face told him she was scared. But she wasn't looking at him.

Will looked up, and saw Charlie next to a body. It lay next to the tree the horde of undead demons had been gathered around. Charlie wasn't touching the mangled figure. He only kneeled next to it, his face buried into the palms of his hands. Holly turned around, away from the body. Will looked at the lower half of it, remembering those neon-colored sneakers. They were unmistakable.

It was Reece.

Beside the teen's body lay a knife, its blade stained with blood. So much blood and pieces of the kid's insides surrounded the distorted corpse that there was no way to tell if the knife had been used in self-defense, or if Reece had used it to end his own life before the creatures got to him. Will hoped it had been the latter.

Will turned around and went to Holly, who still faced the direction they'd come from, her back turned from Reece's body. He put his hand on her shoulder, which startled her.

"We have to go," Will whispered. "Dylan and Mary Beth are still out here somewhere."

Sniffing uncontrollably, Holly looked up to him, her eyes filled, and nodded.

Will said, "Come on, let's—"

A scream and two gunshots jerked Will's head around.

They'd come in succession, from deep in the woods.

Without a second thought or looking back, Will ran.

***

Mary Beth screamed again.

Dylan, in such terrified awe of his surroundings, practically didn't hear her.

They'd come across a tree stump and decided to stop and rest. They'd only been sitting down for a couple of minutes before, almost as if the things had drawn up the attack, a group of Empties had surrounded them.

Snarls came from every direction. At first, they'd just seen the creatures in front of them. Then, when Dylan grabbed Mary Beth's hand and turned around, more of the things had flanked them from behind. He wasn't sure where they'd come from, or how he hadn't heard them. All he knew was that he and his friend were trapped, sitting on a tree stump in the middle of nowhere.

The gun trembled in the boy's hand, as he found himself at a loss for what to do. Confusion and panic filled his young mind. He tried to bring his hand up and point it at one of the creatures, but he couldn't. And even if he did, he'd just used his last two bullets.

"It's just like Susan," Mary Beth mumbled through tears.

Dylan just looked at her, and even though she didn't look up, he could see that she sensed him looking upon her.

"The woods. Home Base. I'm gonna die just like her."

Looking around him, it all made sense what she was trying to say. In fact, it was exactly as Dylan had imagined it when Mary Beth had told her own story about The Fall. The tree stump they sat on now was just like the one Mary Beth and her sister, Susan, had called Home Base. He looked to her again and saw the quit in her eyes. She'd given up.

Dylan wasn't going to let her go that easy.

He remembered the knife he had with him, and reached down to grip the handle. The Empties had moved only moments away from being within arms' lengths of the two children. Dylan stood up and drew the knife.

"You're not dying out here," he said.

The boy was about to lunge at one of the creatures when he heard his name.

"Dylan!"

He looked beyond one of the creatures, which had now turned around, and saw Will running toward them, waving his arms down toward the ground. Dylan cocked his head.

"Get down!" Will yelled, readying his rifle from behind his back.

Dylan's eyes widened, and he pulled Mary Beth off of the tree stump and down to the ground with him. Bullets raced by overhead, and he felt the Empties' blood splash down onto him. Mary Beth screamed, and Dylan himself moaned in fear, quaking. He heard the creatures hit the ground all around him as bullets mowed them down.

After what seemed like much more time had passed, the gunfire ceased. With it, Mary Beth's scream became a shudder.

Dylan looked up to see the creatures all around him, their bodies lying tangled, limbs twisted like they'd just been tossed aside. He looked up further and his eyes met Will's. Holly and Charlie stood on either side of him, and Holly was the first to run to him.

Dylan stood all the way up and hugged Holly. He buried his face of tears into her chest as she ran her hand through his hair.

"I'm so glad you're okay," Holly said.

When Dylan pulled away, Will was standing beside Holly. Will smiled, and embraced Dylan.

"Thank you," Dylan said.

They pulled away from each other, and Will rummaged the boy's hair and smiled.

Turning around, Dylan checked on Mary Beth, who'd taken a seat on the tree stump again. Her face was pale, blank with shock. A combination of dirt, blood, and tears covered her face. Her hair swooped down over her right eye, tangled and matted.

Dylan took a step toward her and said, "Mary Beth, are you —"

The Empty appeared over her shoulder so fast. It rose up from behind the tree stump, growled, and then grabbed her by the shoulders. It tried to pull her back, but she fought it, slapping at the thing's decrepit grip.

"No!" Dylan yelled, and he lunged at the creature.

Right as the thing was about to bite Mary Beth on her shoulder, Dylan blocked it with his own arm.

He screamed as the creature bit into his flesh and grabbed onto him.

"Move!" Will yelled at Mary Beth.

When she didn't, Charlie ran over and swept the young girl off of the stump.

The Empty dug deeper into Dylan's arm, tearing flesh from bone. Dylan's shrill was so high-pitched, it cut through his own ears. He watched in agony as Will lunged at the beast and drove his knife into its skull. The grip of its teeth loosened, and it fell to the ground.

Dylan's vision doubled as he tried to look down at his forearm and see the damage the thing had done. Blood spilled from the wound, his flesh dangling off his limb. Dylan became lightheaded, and he had started to lose his balance when Will caught him.

Will put Dylan on his knees and set his arm down on the tree stump. He removed his shirt, forming it into a cylindrical shape.

"Hold his arm down," Will said to someone. "And give me that."

Dylan looked up, and with blurred vision, saw Charlie handing a large blade over to Will. Dylan then looked over to see Holly at his side, holding down his arm.

The taste of iron in Dylan's mouth was replaced by sweaty cotton as Will placed the t-shirt in his mouth.

"Bite down, hard," Will said.

Dylan tried to scream through the shirt as one of the others held his arm down against the tree stump. He felt every ounce of energy he had leaving him, and his vision started to go black.

Will said, "I'm so sorry."

The last thing Dylan saw before he blacked out was Will above him, his machete raised over his head.

EPILOGUE

She came walking out of the Welcome Center, her hair up in a ponytail. He wondered what it would look like if she let it flow down her smooth shoulders. That dark hair. He hadn't seen one like her yet.

He had to have her.

She walked down the sidewalk, looking off into the manufactured trees that had been planted to make the State Welcome Center seem more inviting. He didn't move from his hiding spot behind the railing aside the highway; he just continued to watch her. The way she walked, it excited him. The others, they'd want to use her for their stupid games. There'd be plenty of time for that, but he hoped he'd get to play his own games with her first. He bit his bottom lip, thinking of the possibilities.

The dark-haired girl reached the end of the sidewalk, and then she turned around. In a way, he wanted her to look his way. He knew it would be nearly impossible for her to see him, well as he was hidden. But it would be almost like a tease. He loved to be teased.

He felt the slow dance begin in his pants just as the door to the Welcome Center opened again, drawing his attention away from the pretty young girl.

A man walked out. He reached to the sky, stretching, before turning toward the ground like he was going to puke. He then covered up his face, and ran toward Sexy Dark Hair.

"You've gotta be fuckin' kiddin' me," he mumbled.

This asshole, walking out of the building and almost throwing up for no reason, he would die. And it would be fun. Slow and fun. And painful.

The two-way radio hissed.

"You see anything? Over," a man said from the other end of the radio.

Licking his lips, eyes locked on the girl, he waited to respond. Cock Blocker hadn't ruined his fun so much to where he couldn't take a moment to admire her a little more. But when the radio hissed again, asking if he was there, he finally shook himself from his dream and put the radio up to his mouth.

"Yeah," he said. "Yeah, we've got some live ones here. Let's get ready to wrangle 'em up."

AUTHOR'S NOTE

Thanks for reading Empty Bodies 4: Open Roads.

I wanted to just take a moment and thank you for reading this series. It has been so much fun for me to write, and I feel very attached to all these characters. The whole thing has been a great experience for me, and I've learned so much about writing and storytelling.

The journey isn't over quite yet, as I've still got two more books to share with you. I've been working on Empty Bodies 5: Damnation, and can tell you with a lot of confidence that is probably going to end up being my favorite book in the entire series. The storyline that the epilogue you just read leads into has been brutally entertaining for me to write, and I know you'll love reading it as much as I have enjoyed writing it.

Again, thank you so much. Writing books is a lot of hard work, and happens over many hours spent alone, so it is very fulfilling to know that people are enjoying the story.

Now, strap in, and get ready for the penultimate title!

Zach Bohannon

November 27th, 2015

ACKNOWLEDGEMENTS

Thank you to all the readers who've come along this journey with me!

Thank you to The Empties!

Thanks, as always, to Johnny Digges for another great cover, and to Jennifer Collins for another fantastic edit.

ABOUT THE AUTHOR

Something about the dark side of life has always appealed to me. Whether I experience it through reading and watching horror or listening to my favorite heavy metal bands, I have been forever fascinated with the shadow of human emotion.

While in my 20's, I discovered my passion to create through playing drums in two heavy metal bands: Kerygma and Twelve Winters. While playing in Twelve Winters (a power metal band with a thrash edge fronted by my now wife Kathryn), I was able to indulge myself in my love of writing by penning the lyrics for all our music. My love of telling a story started here, as many of the songs became connected to the same concept and characters in one way or another.

Now in my 30's, my creative passion is being passed to willing readers through the art of stories. While I have a particular fascination for real life scenarios, I also love dark fantasy. So, you'll find a little bit of everything in my stories, from zombies to serial killers, angels and demons to mindless psychopaths, and even ghosts and parallel dimensions.

My influences as a writer come primarily from the works of Clive Barker, Stephen King, and Blake Crouch in the written form; the beautifully dark, rich lyrics of Mikael Akerfeldt from the band Opeth; and an array of movies, going back to the root of my fascination at a young age with 70's and 80's slasher films such as *Halloween, Friday the 13th,* and *The Texas Chainsaw Massacre.*

I live in Nashville, Tennessee with my wife Kathryn, our daughter Haley, and our German Shepherd Guinness. When I'm not writing, I enjoy playing hockey, watching hockey and football, cycling, watching some of my favorite television shows and movies, and, of course, reading.

Connect with me online:

Website: www.zachbohannon.com
Subscribe: http://bit.ly/zbbjoin
Facebook: http://www.facebook.com/zbbwrites
Pinterest: http://www.pinterest.com/zbbwrites
Twitter: @zachbohannon32
Instagram: @zachbohannon

Made in the USA
Monee, IL
23 August 2020